PENG

#YOU

#YOUDUNNIT

NICCI FRENCH
TIM WEAVER
ALASTAIR GUNN

PENGUIN BOOKS

PENGUIN BOOKS

Published by the Penguin Group
Penguin Books Ltd, 80 Strand, London WC2C ORL, England
Penguin Group (USA) Inc., 375 Hudson Street, New York, New York 10014, USA
Penguin Group (Canada), 90 Eglinton Avenue East, Suite 700, Toronto, Ontario, Canada M4M 2M3
(a division of Pearson Penguin Canada Inc.)
Penguin Ireland, 25 St Stephen's Green, Dublin 2, Ireland (a division of Penguin Books Ltd)
Penguin Group (Australia), 250 Camberwell Road,
Camberwell, Victoria 3124, Australia (a division of Pearson Australia Group Pty Ltd)
Penguin Books India Pvt Ltd, 11 Community Centre, Panchsheel Park,
New Delhi – 110 017, India
Penguin Group (NZ), 67 Apollo Drive, Rosedale, North Shore 0632, New Zealand
(a division of Pearson New Zealand Ltd)
Penguin Books (South Africa) (Pty) Ltd, Block D, Rosebank Office Park, 181 Jan Smuts Avenue,
Parktown North, Gauteng, Johannesburg 2193, South Africa

Penguin Books Ltd, Registered Offices: 80 Strand, London WC2C ORL, England

www.penguin.com

Published in Penguin Books 2013
001

Copyright © Joined-Up Writing 2013
Copyright © Tim Weaver 2013
Copyright © Alastair Gunn 2013

All rights reserved

The moral right of the authors has been asserted

Printed in England

Except in the United States of America, this book is sold subject
to the condition that it shall not, by way of trade or otherwise, be lent,
re-sold, hired out, or otherwise circulated without the publisher's
prior consent in any form of binding or cover other than that in
which it is published and without a similar condition including this
condition being imposed on the subsequent purchaser

ISBN:: 978-1-405-91653-0

www.greenpenguin.co.uk

Penguin Books is committed to a sustainable
future for our business, our readers and our planet.
This book is made from Forest Stewardship
Council™ certified paper.

Contents

The Brief
vii

The Case Files
ix

The Following
Nicci French
1

Disconnection
Tim Weaver
37

Hashtag, Bodybag
Alastair Gunn
85

The Brief

When Penguin and Specsavers decided to ask crime fans in the twitter community to contribute plot devices for a crime thriller story, what would the results be? Candlesticks and libraries, clichés more suited to a boardgame than a short story? Or would the ideas be far more obscure and imaginative?

And how would three very different crime authors interpret this framework? Would they inevitably write the same tale, or would the stories hanging around these plot markers be inventive and intriguing, personal to each author?

To answer these questions, we approached Nicci French, Tim Weaver and Alastair Gunn, hoping they would participate in the #Youdunnit experiment: take these crowdsourced plot points and prompts and use them to write a short story.

How could they say no?

'We're looking forward to seeing ideas from crime readers for the #Youdunnit experiment. To have much of the plotting taken out of our hands could be a blessing or a curse – time will tell!'

Nicci French

#Youdunnit began, and we were thrilled by the response from readers. Over a thousand tweets and 675 ideas contributed to the debate, choosing not just the plot, but even the titles and cover design. A week later, we distilled all the proposals down to a single framework to pass to these ever-more-anxious authors. To keep those creative juices flowing we asked that the authors used the crowdsourced ideas wherever possible. Whilst not compulsory to use them all, we were keen that the key details were incorporated when the opportunity arose. Oh, and we gave them just ten days . . .

We think the results are fantastic: three rich, intricate and unique stories. But it's you, the crime-reading public, who chose the barebones of them, so we'd love to know what you think of the results.

We hope you enjoy the pages that follow. Let us know what you think, using #Youdunnit.

The Case Files

The Murder

MURDER TYPE: The followers of one twitter account are murdered, one by one.

MURDER LOCATION: Disused railway station

ITEM LEFT ON SCENE: Bicycle chain

VICTIM NAME: Jo

VICTIM DETAILS: 27 y/o old female University student

SETTING: Small town in autumn. The town is surrounded by industry and there's a lake on the road out of town.

The Hero

HERO NAME: Lucinda Berrington

AGE: 28 y/o female

JOB: Travel photographer

NATIONALITY: UK, Dorset

MARITAL STATUS: Recently fallen in love in a neurotic and distracting way

FASHION STYLE: quirky/python-skin cowboy boots

FASHION ITEM: Specs

BODY TYPE: 5ft10

INTERESTS: Art deco / break dance /Progressive rock from seventies

PERSONALITY TRAITS: Sleeps badly

PAST JOBS: IT geek that had own company providing IT support

LIFE EVENT: She won a spelling bee aged 11

EDUCATION: Left school after A levels

OTHER CHARACTERISTICS: Border collie for company.

The Appearance

FRONT COVER ITEM: A discarded bicycle
FRONT COVER COLOURS: Black and red

The Following

NICCI FRENCH

@FrenchNicci

Idea for murder victim: person who thought of #youdunnit short story crimescene. Idea for suspects: @TimWeaverBooks, @alastair_gunn and us.

It had been four weeks and three days now, but sometimes I forgot that she was dead. A thought would flit through my head and I'd want to share it with her. I would read something in the papers that made me angry and wonder what she would make of it. I would take a photograph and ask myself what Jo would think. I would overhear a conversation and tuck it away to repeat to her later. Several times a week, I would feel like calling her to say, I've seen a dress that would look great on you; there's a film we've got to go to together; you'll never guess who I met; I'm down; I'm happy; I've fallen in love and what shall I do? Her number was still on my mobile. She was in my old address book, a patchwork of different flats where she'd lived over the years, scrawlings and crossings out. Her face was stored in my camera and on my computer and in my memory. But she was gone. We wouldn't grow old knowing each other: partners, jobs, babies, wrinkles, grey hairs. We wouldn't be batty ninety-year-olds tottering towards the end together, as we'd always promised each other, laughing as we said it because who in their twenties can imagine being ninety?

It wasn't just that Jo had died; she had been killed. Perhaps that was why I caught myself believing that she was alive and that when I turned a corner she would be there, small and strong and wry-faced, or that it was her looking out of the window of a bus as it lumbered past. Because it was simply inconceivable: someone had murdered my dear, stubborn, buoyant and rather grumpy friend.

She was a cyclist. She cycled to work and for exercise and for fun; carelessly, recklessly, in electric colours and no helmet. I thought she risked being hit by a van. But she had been on the cycle path, far from any traffic. It was a converted railway line. She was ambushed, dragged into one of the abandoned old stations. Strangled. Her body was still in the morgue. One of the papers – and for a couple of weeks she had been in every paper, at first on the front page with her face across four columns, using a photo I'd taken last summer; then inside, the headlines shrinking – had mentioned something about a bicycle chain. I tried not to imagine it, but I couldn't stop it: the thought of her struggling, suffering, knowing what was happening to her.

But that morning, the morning it all began, I hadn't been dreaming that Jo was being killed. I had been dreaming that she was still alive. She was holding a wicker basket of plum tomatoes and wearing ballet shoes. She didn't look like Jo at all, but with the logic of dreams I knew that it was her. She asked if I wasn't glad to see her, but before I could reply, before I could hug her, I woke. The sun was shining through the half-opened curtains and I could hear birds singing outside and a tractor in the distance. It was autumn, a time of stubble fields and misty dawns. For a moment I couldn't remember where I was, nor who it was lying next to me, one arm flung across my body, a shock of dark hair, a beaky nose, unshaven, his mouth slightly open, his chest rising and falling with his sleeping breath.

I stared at him, at the room, the flung clothes and the empty bottle of wine beside the bed. I had met Connor the day before Jo died. I couldn't seem to disentangle the two events in my mind.

There was a scratching at the door, which opened, and I saw a wet black nose, two brown sad eyes, a hopeful wagging tail. Filby's claws clattered over the bare boards towards me. He was carrying one of my socks. My phone rang on the bedside table. Connor stirred, muttered something, groaned. It was only just after seven. I reached my hand across him, found the phone and brought it to my ear.

'Is that Lucinda Berrington?'

For a moment the name took me by surprise. Only teachers, my mother when she was cross, and people inspecting my passport ever called me Lucinda. Lucy, Luce, Lu.

'Who is this?'

'My name is Detective Inspector McMahon. West Dorset.'

Suddenly I was awake. What had I done? What was I guilty of?

'What is it?' I asked. 'What's happened?'

'Fuck it, Lucy, your knees are bizarrely sharp,' Connor announced loudly, distinctly.

'Sorry?' said the detective.

'Nothing. What's this about?'

'I need to talk to you.'

'Why?' My mind raced. Had I been speeding? But a detective wouldn't ring me at seven in the morning if I'd simply been speeding. Had Filby been chasing sheep?

No; he was a border collie but he was terrified of sheep.

'Is someone dead? My brother?' I asked. I saw Jo's face, eyebrows raised. Connor sat up and put his hand on the small of my back.

'Your brother?'

'Or my mother?'

'Nothing like that. It would be best if I came and talked to you. How about this morning?'

'This morning?' I repeated stupidly.

'Nine o'clock.'

I knew I hadn't been speeding because I never speed. I don't use my mobile phone while driving. I didn't steal from sweetshops when I was a girl. I've almost never taken illegal drugs. I'm not a particularly moral person. I'm a person who's particularly unnerved by the idea of being caught. So when the two detectives arrived – the man on the phone had brought a female colleague – my entire house took on a guilty atmosphere, a den of crime where stolen goods were stored, fire regulations violated and conspiracies planned. And then I realized.

'Is this about Jo?'

DI McMahon turned round. He had been looking at a photograph on the wall, one of mine. It was a wrecked ship on the skeleton coast in Namibia. He had a faintly suspicious expression, as if the picture had been obtained through dubious means.

'Why do you say that?'

'She was my friend. She was murdered. Is it about her?'

'In a way,' said McMahon.

The other detective was also looking at the pictures on

the wall, as if she were in a gallery. The two detectives looked like different generations. He was suited and brushed like the manager of a supermarket. She was younger, with dark, curly hair. She looked like she wasn't long out of university. She stopped in front of a photograph of an Icelandic glacier.

'Is this yours?'

'Yes.'

'Do you do this for a living?'

It sounded like an accusation.

'Yes.'

McMahon pulled an LP out of the shelves. The gatefold sleeve opened out like a concertina.

'*Yes*?' he said.

'That's what they're called.'

'Is this a double?' he said.

'A triple,' I replied. 'Live.'

'Bloody hell. You listen to this?'

It sounded like an aggravating offence.

'Sometimes. Late at night.'

The woman was staring at another photograph.

'You must get to travel a lot.'

'Well, you don't find glaciers and sand dunes in Dorset.'

'My boyfriend takes photographs.'

My heart sank. It was going to be one of those discussions.

'I think almost everyone in the world takes photographs,' I said.

'He's good at it.'

I didn't reply.

'I haven't introduced my colleague,' said McMahon.

'Detective Constable Webster. She has some questions for you.'

'About Jo?'

'Can we take this one step at a time?'

We arranged ourselves awkwardly in my small living room: me in an armchair, DC Webster in the other armchair, McMahon on an uncomfortable wooden chair. He placed it so he was facing me, with Webster to one side. Filby tried to lick his hand and he made a grimace of distaste and moved away. He nodded at Webster.

'This is about Jo Goodman,' she said.

'It was terrible. I thought you'd find someone straight away.'

'We're making progress,' said McMahon.

'So why are you here?'

'Tell us about your online presence,' said Webster.

'My what?'

'Don't you understand the words?'

'Yes, I understand the words. My online presence: I've got a website, like every other photographer in the world. If you want to buy a print, you can Google me and go there. The prices are very reasonable.'

'What else?'

'The usual. Facebook, but I don't use it much any more.'

'Why?'

'Because I'm not fifteen years old.'

'Anything else?'

'I think that's about it.'

'What about Twitter?'

'What about it?'

'You have a Twitter account.'

'Sort of.'

'That's wasn't a question,' said Webster. 'You have a Twitter account.'

'I'd forgotten about it. I've probably got about nine followers.'

'Twenty-three.'

'Really? Still, it's not exactly Stephen Fry, is it?'

'It was twenty-two. It's twenty-three now because I'm following you.'

'You won't find it worth your while. I've only done one tweet.'

'Two,' said Webster, looking down at her notes. 'The first said, "This is a tweet", and the second said, "The biggest sand dune in the world". It read like there should be a photo attached, but there wasn't.'

'I couldn't work out how to do it. Then I lost interest. As you've noticed.'

'So who are your followers?' asked Webster.

'I don't know. I haven't checked. You can see, can't you?'

'Your friend Josephine Goodman was one of them.'

'That's right,' I said. I had a sudden memory that felt like a toothache, the sort of toothache that starts in your jaw and then you feel it right through your body. 'We were having a drink. I mentioned that I was going to set up a Twitter account and I doubted whether anyone would actually follow me. She said that she would follow me if I'd follow her.'

'But you didn't follow her.'

'No. I didn't.' I looked at DC Webster, and Webster and McMahon looked at each other, and neither of them replied. 'Look,' I continued, 'there are a lot of things I didn't do online. I've joined all kinds of social networks and never used them. I've created email addresses and forgotten about them.' There was another silence. 'Why does this even matter? Why do you care how active I was on bloody Twitter?'

'Your Twitter followers,' said Webster, 'were they friends of yours?'

'I don't know,' I said. 'I forgot about it almost immediately.' I stopped and thought for a moment. 'Lynne. Lynne Wells. She was at my school.'

Webster looked down at her notes.

'I have a Lynne Grainger.'

'Grainger? Oh yes. She got married and changed her name. I always think of women by their real names.'

'One of those?' said McMahon.

'I'm sorry?'

I heard a door slamming shut upstairs and then the shower running and Connor singing loudly. McMahon looked at me as if he had discovered a dirty secret.

'Can we get on to what this is about?' I said.

'What we're trying to establish', said Webster, 'is whether you and your Twitter followers formed some sort of group.'

'No,' I said. 'We're not a group.'

'Like a fan club.'

'I don't have fans.'

'People who like your photographs.'

'It doesn't work like that.'

'What about enemies?' said McMahon.

'Enemies?'

'Don't photographers have enemies?'

'One, I get commissions for travel pieces. I go to beautiful places and try to make them look beautiful, that's all. Two, if I did have enemies, which I don't think I do, or not in the way you mean, they wouldn't just follow me on Twitter and not do anything. And three, Jo and Lynne are – or were – friends of mine. So I don't understand what you're getting at.'

Webster looked down at her notes again.

'Michelle Horne,' she said.

'Who?'

'She's one of your followers.'

'I've never heard of her.'

'Take a moment,' said McMahon. 'Try to remember.'

'There's nothing to remember.'

'Catherine Calder,' said Webster.

'Is this another of my followers?'

'Yes.'

'It doesn't ring a bell.'

'Her name before she married was Catherine Rigby.'

'No. Sorry.'

'Have you any idea why either of these women might have decided to follow you?'

'I don't even know who they are.'

'Is there a particular photograph of yours that's famous or controversial?'

'I wish. I'd love to have taken one of those iconic pictures that everyone remembers and magazines keep wanting to reproduce, but mainly what I do is unspoilt beaches, which will appear in a magazine and encourage people to go and spoil them.'

'So you've no idea?'

'Probably these people saw my credit on a photo somewhere and then wanted to find out more. Then they followed me on Twitter – it must have been a pretty disappointing experience. What is it with these women anyway?'

Webster looked down at her notes.

'Your friend, Josephine Goodman, died a month ago on the twenty-third of August.'

'Josephine,' I said. 'It sounds odd to hear her called that.'

'Michelle Horne lived about thirty miles away in Benfleet. Two weeks earlier, on the twelfth of August, she was found dead at her home. She'd been strangled in a particularly violent assault. She was throttled with a bicycle chain that was left at the scene. Does that sound familiar?'

'Yes, it does,' I said faintly.

'There's more,' McMahon continued. 'Miss Horne was about to be married. A few days later, her fiancé committed suicide. He said he couldn't live without her. People forget that. When there's a murder, there's always more than one victim.'

'What about the other woman?'

'She lives in Horsted, just up the road. Lived. Didn't you see the papers?'

'I don't often read the papers.'

'On the morning of September the fourteenth, she was discovered by a woman walking her dog. Her body was found behind a bus shelter outside the village. Strangled. Bicycle chain.'

'I see,' I said, although I didn't at all.

'What do you see?'

I had to pause for a moment. Think.

'It sounds like a message.'

'Yes. But what kind of message?'

'I mean, a bicycle chain isn't the first weapon that comes to hand. Why would someone . . . ?' I stopped. I thought again of Jo's face, her smile.

'Leave that to us,' said McMahon. 'The fact is, these women don't know each other. They live in the same vicinity, but not especially near to each other. They don't do similar jobs or have similar interests. They are fairly close in age – twenty-four, twenty-seven, thirty-six – but that doesn't seem very significant. To our eyes they don't even look much alike. But they all follow you on Twitter.'

For a moment I felt a lurching sensation of vertigo. I found it difficult to think clearly.

'But people follow lots of people on Twitter. There are probably other people they all follow as well.'

'They don't,' said Webster. 'I've checked. They don't even all follow Stephen Fry. But they all follow you. That's the only thing we've got and we don't understand it.'

'We want you to be absolutely clear,' said McMahon. 'Did any of them approach you about something? Is there a connection with one or all of them that you'd rather keep hidden?'

'What do you mean by that?'

'Whatever it is, it doesn't matter. We'll be discreet. We just need to find this monster.'

'I'll be as clear as you want,' I said. 'Jo was my friend. I know it makes no sense, but I know nothing about the others. Nothing at all.'

The two detectives looked at each other and stood up. As I led them outside, McMahon turned to me.

'You're the focus of this somehow,' he said, 'and that's not a safe place to be.' He took a card from his pocket and handed it to me. 'So if you think of anything or notice anything, anything at all.'

'What do you mean, not safe?'

'We don't know,' he said.

The two detectives looked round at the newly cut field on the other side of the road.

'When I see a haystack,' said Webster, 'I think of needles.'

'What?' said McMahon.

'Needles. Needles in haystacks.'

'With a good metal detector', I said, 'you'd find a needle in two minutes. Straw.'

'What?' said McMahon again.

'A haystack would be a good place to hide a piece of straw.'

He looked baffled.

'Call us,' he said, 'if you think of anything, anything at all.'

They left and I was alone, standing in the middle of the room with an ache in my chest, as if the floor was suddenly a choppy sea beneath me. I sat down and put my head in my hands. Three women had been killed with a bicycle chain. They had all followed me on Twitter. It was both ominous and senseless. And then the words of the police officers returned to me: 'Not a safe place.'

Sitting there, it seemed as though a stain was spreading through me. I concentrated on the stark, incomprehensible facts: women have been murdered and they follow you on Twitter. And then, like letting in the inky darkness,

I felt the question form in my mind and clarify. Or is it that women have been murdered *because* they follow you? If what they all had in common was me – even the ones I didn't know and had never heard of – then somehow I was the cause. I could almost feel the thoughts hissing inside me, useless and urgent. What had I done or said or thought or photographed that could have set this off? If Jo had been alive, I would have picked up the phone right then to talk to her and ask her advice. I tried to imagine what she would have said, but all I could think about was that she wasn't there to say it. She was dead. Had she died because of me?

I heard Connor's footsteps on the stairs. He was a lecturer at the university. Politics. Term hadn't started yet. I'd said that I thought the vacation was when academics did research and wrote books, and he had looked evasive. I had met him at a gig I'd gone to with a group of friends. He had stood next to me, and once or twice we'd bumped against each other in the jostle of the crowd. He had smiled at me, had steadied me when someone pushed violently from behind. And then had said into my ear, as if we were a couple already, 'This isn't much good, is it? Let's go and get a drink.' Although I don't do that sort of thing, I went, just like that. And although I never have one-night stands, I took him home later that night and let him kiss me, undress me slowly, lay me on the bed, looking at me as if I was the most beautiful person he had ever seen. Usually I am the one who does the looking, watching the world through a lens, perhaps hiding behind it – that's what Jo used to say anyway – but Connor gazed at me, gazed into me, appraised me. There seemed no place to hide. I didn't know if I liked or hated this. Certainly it scared me.

He came into the room, pulling a T-shirt over his torso. I looked at his flat white stomach disappearing, his head emerging, damp dark hair and hooded dark eyes.

'Hello, my gorgeous,' he said, putting his hand on my cheek, sending that familiar shiver of pleasure through me. 'I'll make a big pot of coffee and you can tell me what they wanted. What crime have you committed?'

I told him and watched the way his eyes seemed to grow darker. He seemed – what was the word? – impressed. He let out a low whistle. He took my hand and held it between his own, twisting my thumb ring.

'Well?' I asked. 'What do you think?'

'I think,' he said slowly. 'I think it's quite extraordinary.'

'What should I do? What does it all mean? You see, I don't even know what the question is. It's just . . .' I searched for a word. 'Ghastly.'

'Are you scared?'

'I don't even know. Churned up. I feel dizzy and unreal.'

He took me in his arms. I smelt the shampoo on him and felt his stubble scrape my cheek. He was my stranger. I knew he loved the same kind of music as me and that he liked to cook and to drink red wine and walk along the cliff tops when it was windy. But I didn't know his family; I didn't know his friends; I knew almost nothing about his past.

I broke away from him and went to stand by the window, feeling cold and shivery, even though the day was mild and the morning sun slanted across the fields and hedgerows.

'Let's start by looking at your Twitter account,' he said.

I don't know why I hadn't thought of that. I fetched my laptop and went to Twitter, which I never use even though all my friends tell me I should, and then to 'Connect' so that I could see the activity on my page.

As I had told McMahon, and McMahon had told me, I don't have many followers. Twenty-three, including him, and three of them were dead, although their names were still there. I scrolled down. I knew Jo, of course, and, vaguely, Lynne Grainger, née Wells. A few minutes ago I had heard of Michelle Horne and Catherine Calder. The other names were unfamiliar, some of them obviously weren't real names at all. I stared at them. I stared at the images beside their tags: thumb-sized faces or sometimes logos or cartoons. I saw that a refuge for stray dogs was following me, and a local restaurant. They were safe enough. There was even someone from New Zealand.

'This isn't . . .' I began, and then a message pinged onto the screen, sent by a Geraldine Finch, whose photo showed her to be middle-aged, plump and smiling.

'Scarifying visit from police,' it read. 'Anyone else?'

Connor looked pleased.

'This is interesting.'

'What?'

'The police are visiting your followers. They've gone from you to this woman. We can keep track of it.'

We did keep track of it, all through that strange day. It was like seeing a virus take hold. Messages came slowly at first, then in a strengthening stream of exclamations and alarms that fed off each other. I could almost feel the panic mounting. Questions whirred: Who knew each other? Who knew the women who had been murdered? Where were they based? How did the killer find out where they lived? Was it significant that they had all been local to me? Many of the tweets were addressed to me directly. I had no answer.

'What shall I do?'

'Reply,' said Connor.

'And say what?'

'What do you want to say?'

I stood up and paced the room. I'd been inside most of the day and felt stifled, itchy with inaction and a sense that something was coming.

'I think I should suggest that we all meet.'

'Really?' He raised his eyebrows at me, approving.

'There's got to be a reason,' I said. 'Something we know or share. If we all get together, then maybe something will emerge, some pattern. Not the woman in New Zealand, obviously, or the dog refuge or the restaurant.'

Of my nineteen living followers, thirteen were actual individuals. Three of them lived a long way off, in Wellington, Vienna and Ghent. Nine out of the ten remaining said that they would like to meet up as soon as possible. The tenth – a doctor living in Newcastle who, it turned out in a message broken up into multiple tweets, had once seen a picture of mine in a magazine – said he wouldn't come because he was a man and therefore assumed that he wasn't in danger. He wished everyone luck and added that the photograph he had seen by me was of a rainforest in Costa Rica – somewhere he had always wanted to go. The three other men then also dropped out.

By just before midnight, it was arranged. In two days' time – a Sunday – five strangers and an old acquaintance of mine from school would come to my house at midday. One of them was driving from Wales and another from near Sheffield. I'd also invited Catherine Calder's husband, and the brother of Michelle Horne, as representatives of the dead.

'I'd better make lunch,' I said dubiously.

'Let me do that.'

'Really?'

'Yes, Luce, really. I want to be here to see them all.'

I scowled at him. 'You're enjoying this.'

He handed me a glass of whisky. The rawness of it caught me in the back of the throat.

'I'm riveted,' he acknowledged. 'But also . . .'

'Also?'

'I'm not going to let you die.'

For some reason, my eyes stung; perhaps it was the whisky. I tried to smile. 'Thank you.'

'What would I do without you?'

I couldn't tell if he was being ironic or sincere. I could never tell. Even in bed, even when his hand was in my hair and he was leaning over me, staring into me, I couldn't.

'That sounds like a line from a song. I don't know, Connor, what would you do?'

'I'm not going to find out.'

He made a large Mediterranean tart and salads and bought wine and apple juice as well. He wore an apron and sang loudly as he cooked, every so often breaking off to go into the garden for a cigarette. It was as if we were having a party, a reunion of people who had never met. I felt tired because I'd been sleeping badly and, ridiculously,

I worried about what to wear. I didn't want to look too weird, and all the clothes in my wardrobe suddenly seemed like garments for a fancy dress party: the fake python-skin cowboy boots for a Western theme, the leather trousers straight out of *Grease*, and a red satin shirt like a vamp's outfit in a *film noir*, where no one is entirely innocent, and everyone has a guilty secret and shady past. I pulled a pair of jeans from the back of my cupboard and a grey canvas top I often wear on shoots because it has lots of pockets. I tied my hair back and didn't wear make-up. I took out my nose stud. If I'd owned any, I would have put on glasses to make me seem more respectable, more serious. Because I had a horrible feeling that everyone, however unconsciously, would be blaming me. I was obscurely blaming myself. I looked into the mirror and saw my pale face, my dark hair, my heavy brow and the fierceness of my gaze. I didn't look sweet and pure at all.

At first it was a bit like a party – one of those parties where the people you barely know, and were dubious about inviting, arrive first and stand around in awkward clusters making small talk, eyes darting round to look at new arrivals. I examined them: different ages, colours, heights, types, accents, clothes, laughs, backgrounds. It seemed evident that what we had in common was nothing.

By twenty minutes past midday we were all crammed into my tiny sitting room, perched on chairs and sitting on cushions on the floor in an approximate circle. I pinged a knife onto my glass and everyone instantly fell silent, an ominous hush thick in the room.

'I think', I said, 'that we should start by saying who we are and a bit about ourselves.'

I took out a pen and a notebook. I needed to keep some sort of record of this because I already felt lost. So it began:

Jane Wentworth, forty-eight, living in Leicester, divorced, mother of three teenage sons, nursery teacher, cancer survivor.

Lynne Grainger, twenty-eight, married, pregnant (she beamed at me and patted her belly), working in PR, living in London.

Vivian Morgan, thirty-one, married with a young daughter, living in Cambridge and unemployed.

Fiona Carr, twenty-two, a student studying events management, no regular boyfriend (she cast her eyes sideways at Connor, who was leaning in the doorway, still in his apron).

Geraldine Finch, sixty-three, from Norfolk, no husband or partner and no children, but three dogs and a parrot, and a keen amateur photographer.

Tania Fisk, twenty-seven, living in Weymouth with her partner, working as a speech therapist and, as she said, shit-scared by all of this.

Then there was Michelle's brother, Dan Horne, who was slender, wan, his brown hair tied back in a ponytail. He was coming instead of his sister, Claire. She had meant to come because she was the closest to Michelle, but she was still too distraught. And there was Catherine Calder's husband, Bobby, who worked in a bookshop and whose voice cracked when he introduced himself, so that he had to begin again. A hum of sympathy went round the circle, sympathy mixed with a kind of collective flinching. These two represented the women who had already been picked off.

'And I am here for Jo as well as for myself,' I said. 'She's a close friend.' We all heard the present tense. I put my hand on Filby's coarse back and he lifted his sad brown eyes to me and thumped his tail gently.

I don't know exactly what I expected, and after it was all over I wasn't sure what had really happened. Geraldine was the last to go. She had booked herself on a specific train back to London on her way to Norfolk and she had allowed herself much too much time. When the door finally closed behind her, I was left with a sink full of coffee mugs and plates, a pile of scrawled notes and Connor.

'So what do you think?' he said.

'Wait.'

While Connor checked his phone and did something online that he said was preparation for the beginning of term, I tried to restore the house to the way it had been three hours earlier. I did the washing up. I pushed the chairs back into their proper places. I found a grey cardigan that Vivian Morgan had been wearing when she arrived and folded it. It had moth holes in its sleeves. I picked up the reading glasses that Bobby Calder had left on the side table and put them in the drawer of my desk, promising myself I'd take them back the following day. Someone, I had no idea who, had left a brightly patterned scarf behind. A few of the visitors had gone outside for a cigarette. Only just outside. Cigarette ends and matches are not like compost; they don't melt into the soil. I had to pick them up one by one.

When I was finished, I put the kettle on for coffee and then decided that caffeine wasn't enough. I opened the fridge and there was half a bottle of white wine left over from lunch. I poured myself and Connor a glass each. We walked outside and Filby followed us. It was a beautiful evening, almost hot, as the sun shone against the rear of the cottage. But there was a chill beneath it. You could feel that this was autumn now, not summer, and that winter was somewhere in the distance.

'So?' I said.

Connor took a sip of wine and grinned.

'I think he killed the wrong women,' he said.

It suddenly felt like the sun had gone away. I shivered.

'You think all this is funny?' I said. 'Well, fuck you. I'll do this on my own.'

I walked back inside, sat down at the table and started to look at the notes I'd taken. Connor sat down beside me. His face looked flushed.

'That came out wrong,' he said.

'There is no way it could possibly have come out right.'

'I'm just a guy. When I try to deal with serious emotions, I end up making a joke.'

'You sound proud of it,' I said.

'I'm so not.'

I gestured at my notes.

'Are we going to do this?'

'I want to help you,' he said. 'I want to be part of this.'

'So where do we start?'

Connor found a fresh piece of paper. He looked at my notes and wrote the names of everyone who had been at the meeting.

'They followed you for different reasons,' he said. 'Geraldine just follows any photographer she comes across.

Lynne remembered you from school. Tania saw a picture of yours on a website and clicked on the link. Fiona said she was following anyone who could be a potential contact. Vivian follows more than a thousand people and couldn't remember why she had followed you. Jane was following people in the hope that they would follow her for a charity. You didn't follow any of them, not even your old friend, Lynne. Or Jo, when she was alive. Michelle's brother didn't know why she followed you. Catherine's husband didn't know why she followed you.'

'Lynne's not exactly an old friend.'

'All of them have been interviewed by the police. None of them knew any of the victims.'

'None of them have anything in common.'

'What they have in common is you.'

'Thanks very much. I'm aware of that.'

'You're welcome,' said Connor. 'And the police hinted that you might be in danger, didn't they?'

'They said I was in an unsafe place.'

'Right. But these women are the ones sitting there in Weymouth and Norfolk and wherever else, wondering if they're next.'

'Do you think they blame me?'

'I think they're confused and scared. Tania was especially scared, and yes, I think she blamed you. She kept looking around the house as if there was a curse on it. She was like a sweet little hunted animal.'

I looked at Connor and didn't say anything, but I wondered if there was some way he was actually getting off on this. If he was one of those people who slow down as they drive past a car pile-up, just so they can get a proper look. Most relationships don't get tested like this. But I had things to do, things to think about. I couldn't distract myself with that now.

'It's like a photograph,' I said.

'I don't understand what you mean.'

'I mean it's like the way I see photographs. It's probably to do with being a photographer. Most people, when they see a picture of a starving child or a riot, they just see the events, but I always see what's not in the photograph, which is the person holding the camera. What effect is the photographer having on the event?'

'I'm sorry,' said Connor. 'I don't see the connection.'

'This is the opposite. Everybody's looking at the photographer and not at the photograph.'

'You're going to have to explain this to me.'

'Strip everything away – me, Twitter – and you're left with three deaths: Michelle Horne, Catherine Calder and Jo. Just look at them and nothing else.'

'And?'

'Isn't there an odd one out?'

'You mean that you knew Jo?'

'Michelle Horne. Her death feels different. She was killed in her own home. It was followed by another death.'

'But if you're going to play that game, you can see each of them as the odd one out.' Connor thought for a moment. 'For example, Catherine Calder was the only one who was married. Your friend Jo was the only one who actually tweeted about herself.'

I thought for a moment.

'That's right,' I said.

'So you can see patterns where you want to see patterns.'

'No, I mean that's interesting.'

'It wasn't meant to be interesting. I was making a point.'

'Let's have a look at her tweets again.'

'If you remember, they weren't very significant. It was basically "I've run out of toothpaste" or "should I have coffee or maybe I should have tea".'

I gave him a look.

'OK, OK,' he said and pulled his laptop across the table and tapped on the keyboard.

'There we are,' he said. 'It's mainly her cycling. Sample quote: "Biked the Aldham Trail again. Saw two deer." It's not exactly Montaigne. Thank God for social media.'

Even read out in his sarcastic voice, Jo's casual words almost made me cry, but I forced myself to stop. There'd be time for that later.

'You're wrong,' I said. 'That's very significant.'

There was a slightly amused expression on Connor's face that I didn't like.

'If it's significant, then tell the police. Or better still, leave them to get on with their job.'

'There's nothing to tell them,' I said. 'Not yet. There's someone I need to talk to.'

I didn't need to ask her name. As soon as she opened the door I recognized a face that had been drained and harrowed by grief.

'Claire? My name's Lucy Berrington,' I said.

She was almost unresponsive. She seemed to be on medication.

'I'm so sorry for your loss.'

She looked startled and confused.

'Your brother Dan gave me your address. I hope you don't mind, I wanted to talk to you about Michelle.'

Immediately her eyes became wet and she shook her head.

'I can't . . .' she began and started to cry. I folded her in my arms and felt her own arms around me. I felt stupidly self-conscious, standing on the doorstep of a house on an estate on the edge of a little Dorset town. She was crying and snuffling into my shoulder, and I could feel the dampness through my clothes. Then she moved back and coughed, took a tissue from her pocket and blew her nose.

'I can hardly imagine how awful it must have been,' I said again.

'I still can't believe it. It doesn't seem possible, more like some horrible dream,' she replied.

'And then, not just losing your sister but also your future brother-in-law.'

'That made it even stranger,' she said.

'I'm sure it must have.'

'No, it's not like you think.'

'How do you mean?'

'Michelle wasn't going to go through with it. She'd changed her mind; she'd just told me but he never knew. He died not knowing.'

I had the impulse to hug her again, but then I stopped and stepped back. This changed everything.

For several hours I was overwhelmed. I was so angry I was unable to think. But I had to think, and think clearly. I went back to my house, praying that Connor wouldn't be there. He wasn't, and I remembered him saying that he was planning to bike to his office and work there for a few hours. I put on my running clothes and pounded the lanes for an hour, then I turned onto the footpath that winds round the fields before heading into the woods. At night you can hear the owls screech and small animals rustle in the undergrowth. I pushed myself on until I could feel my legs ache and my lungs hurt; brambles tore at my skin and I welcomed the pain.

I stopped by the little stream and looked down into the clear, fast-running waters. I thought of Jo. I remembered her face when she was concentrating – fierce, almost scowling, her brow creased and the tip of her tongue on her lip. I remembered her on her beloved bike, bent over, small and strong, full of purpose. I remembered her cackling laugh, so clearly that I could almost hear it beneath the burble of the stream. I remembered our holidays together – her atrocious French accent; the way she burnt easily, her nose red and her freckles blotchy; how she looked when she fell asleep on our train journeys, like a child again – and I could feel my anger gradually harden into resolution.

Back at home, I had a shower and made myself a large, strong cup of coffee. There were a couple of messages on my answering machine about work, but that could wait.

I heard the key scrape and turn in the lock. When had I given Connor a key? Since when had he decided he could simply come and go as he pleased? He pushed his bike through the door and leant it against the wall, looking full of energy and mischief.

'So, what are your plans for the day?' he asked.

'I thought I could go to the place where Jo died. I haven't been yet.'

He looked surprised.

'Like visiting a shrine?'

'You could call it that.'

'Will you put flowers at the spot?'

'No.'

'Would you like me to come with you, Luce? I will if it would help.'

'I don't think that would be such a good idea.'

I went alone. A disused railway track that ran through a corridor of trees whose leaves were turning yellow and gold in this beautiful autumn that Jo would not see. An abandoned railway station where her body had been dragged and dumped. I stood in the damp little building that had once housed a ticket office and a waiting room. It smelt of piss and decay. The walls were stained; the windows were broken; there was a mouldy, disintegrating blanket on the floor and a dead pigeon rotting in one corner.

My friend, I thought. Always my friend. It didn't take long.

Later that day, Tania called me, sobbing and hysterical. I told her she wasn't in danger. I said I couldn't explain it right now, but that soon I would.

After another night of insomnia and crazy dreams, I showered vigorously, put on black jeans, my leather jacket and walking boots. Filby could see I was going for a walk, but I couldn't take him with me today, however beseechingly he looked at me.

'You look dangerous,' said Connor approvingly, lying back in bed. He was letting his stubble grow into a beard and it made him look faintly sinister himself.

'Do I?'

'Yes.'

'Good.'

'Where are you off to?'

I didn't answer.

I arrived in good time. After so much turbulence, I felt calm. I had chosen this spot because it was away from the house, but also because Jo and I used to come here sometimes. I had taken several photos of the place, so English and so restful. You could see the landscape stretching away for miles in either direction: a bright patchwork of fields, streams, copses, villages with their small grey churches. I could see smoke coming from some of the chimneys; the year was turning and winter would soon be here.

At last I saw a figure in the distance, approaching me. I waited, not moving until he came fully into view. A nice-looking man, that was what I had thought when I'd first met him. A kind face, lived-in, worn by time and grief.

'Hello, Lucy.' He smiled at me and held out his hand, but I didn't take it, and after a while he dropped his hand and the friendly expression on his face died away, though the smile remained.

'When the police first came to see me,' I said, 'they said something about haystacks. Looking for a needle in a haystack. And I said that needles were easy to find. The thing to hide in a haystack was a piece of straw.'

He looked puzzled.

'What is this? I thought you had something to tell me.'

'My friend Jo,' I said, 'she had lots of plans for her life. She was very resolute. She'd get beaten down by things, but she always got back on her feet. She was valiant and she was kind. She'd recently gone to university to study psychology. Neither of us had gone to university and she had always regretted it and she did something about it. She said it was never too late. She thought that she might be a social worker after that. She had a tabby cat that her step-mother now has. She planned to keep hens. She loved baking bread and cycling. Well, you know about the cycling, of course.'

'I don't know what you're talking about.'

'Jo was your red herring,' I said. 'You killed her to throw the police off the scent. She died because it was . . . *convenient*.'

Bobby Calder's expression didn't change. He held out his hands, palms upwards. 'You're not making any sense,' he said. 'Your mind's been disturbed by grief. I can understand that.'

'I know what happened.'

'What did happen?'

'I visited Claire, the sister of Michelle. The first woman who died. She told me what no one knew: that Michelle was about to break off with her fiancé. She must have told him and so he killed her and then killed himself. Not grief but guilt. Once I knew that, I saw.'

I looked at him closely. I wanted to see his reaction.

'You know,' I said. 'You of all people know that the person who killed Michelle Horne isn't the same person who killed Jo and your wife.'

He didn't reply, but I saw a flicker in his eyes. Where was this going?

'Your bookshop is failing,' I said. 'I went and talked to your staff. You thought that if Catherine died, you would be free of a wife you no longer loved and at the same time be able to get back on your feet financially.'

He smiled. It took a visible effort, but he smiled.

'If you need to tell this ridiculous, offensive fantasy, then tell it to the police.'

'I want to tell it to you,' I said. 'I want you to hear it from me and I wanted to see your face.'

He shrugged.

'I've been thinking', I said, 'about what it must be like to be you. It was something like this, wasn't it? You were sick of your wife. Bloody Catherine.'

'Cath.'

'Bloody Cath. You'd like to be rid of her. Then she tells you that a woman has been murdered. A woman who, like her, follows the same woman on Twitter. And you get an idea. Two women is a coincidence, but three is a pattern. If your wife is suddenly murdered, the police will look very hard at the husband. But if she's the third victim of the bicycle-chain killer, then you're in the clear. You hide a straw in a haystack: a murder in a series of murders. You just needed one more victim.'

'It sounds very clever,' said Bobby Calder. 'A clever story.'

'Doesn't it just? You picked on Jo – it could have been anyone – because of all my followers she was the only one who gave away her whereabouts. She often wrote about cycling the Aldham Trail. It was perfect. You just had to wait.'

He smiled again.

'So why haven't the police suspected that Michelle Horne was killed by her fiancé?'

'I wondered about that and then I realized. He gave you an alibi and you gave him an alibi. Once another murder had been committed using the same method, the fiancé stopped being a suspect.'

'That's funny, Lucy,' he said.

'My name's Lucinda. And it isn't funny.'

'Whatever. I've got to go and open the shop in a minute so, fun as it's been, I need to go now.'

He turned and started to make his way down the slope towards Horsted.

'I'll walk with you,' I said.

'As you wish.'

'Because I haven't finished. You waited there, by the railway tracks, and you saw her cycling towards you. Perhaps she was singing – she often sang when she was on her bike. And you stepped out and knocked her about and then you throttled her with her fucking bike chain, and you threw her body into the old station where it would be found soon enough. You didn't even have to concoct a false alibi, because what was there to connect you to her death? She was killed by the Bike Chain Strangler. I bet you can't say where you were on the day she died, can you?'

'As you point out, I don't have to.'

'Then you just had to wait a week or so before killing your wife as well. Jo was simply an instrument, a bit of camouflage. To kill someone in a fit of jealousy or anger, that's terrible enough. To kill someone because they happen to fit into your plan, like a piece in a board game,

33

that's—' I stopped. I didn't have the words. I only had the picture: the picture of Jo smiling her sweet, dry smile.

We came out onto the small road that led into Horsted and Calder stopped.

'This is where our roads part,' he said.

'That's right,' I said.

'Look.' His tone was almost kind. 'Don't you see. There's absolutely no proof. I've got away with it. If you went to the police with this wild accusation, they would laugh at you.'

We rounded the corner and I saw, as I knew I would, two police cars, lights flashing.

Bobby Calder remained impressively calm. He didn't show any dismay as he approached them, or as he listened to what McMahon had to say. Yes, his business had problems. Yes, there had been certain tensions in his marriage. He admitted that. But he was right. It was a weak case they had against him. It was true, but it was hopelessly weak.

'Where were you on August twenty-third, Mr Calder?'

'I have no idea. Just because she', he gestured towards me, 'has managed to drag you into her paranoid fantasy, doesn't mean that I have to take it seriously too.'

'It would be as well for you if you do take it seriously.'

'Why?'

'We went back to the place where Jo Goodman was murdered.'

McMahon put out his hand and, as if by prior arrangement, Detective Constable Webster handed him a plastic evidence bag. He held it up. Inside was a pair of brown-framed reading glasses. I saw Bobby Calder's mouth open. He looked at them and then at me.

'They're not . . .'

'We have your prescription, and the reference number to the frames,' said McMahon. 'That was very careless. You made it easy for us.'

I saw illumination break over Bobby Calder's features. It was like seeing the tide rolling across the beach, washing into every pool and corner. He turned towards me and took me by the forearm, his fingers pinching into my flesh through the leather jacket.

'You'd better not be around when I get out,' he said.

I walked all the way home. It took two hours, along the footpaths and the hedgerows speckled with blackberries. It was a beautiful evening and the sky turned red as the sun went down. I had a feeling that somewhere, behind it all, Jo was shaking her head in disapproval, and for once I didn't care what she thought. My beloved friend.

Disconnection

TIM WEAVER

@TimWeaverBooks

Reading through the crowdsourced framework for the @Specsavers #Youdunnit short story compo. Never been more terrified.

#SouthAfrica
#2007

#Monday_21_May_2007

There was a boy who used to stand next to the freeway off ramp, about two minutes away from the police station. When he first started to appear, it was to sell flowerpots; tiny terracotta vases, decorated in crude approximations of wild animals. Zill remembered the boy had painted a zebra on one, its black and white body too long, the colours not covering the whole animal. Where the white paint had thinned out, the red of the terracotta had seeped through, so it looked like blood had smeared against the monochrome of its coat.

The boy stopped selling flowerpots after a year and moved on to watermelons, stolen from the fields beyond the city and carried into town in green gauze bags removed from the fruitpacking factories. Shortly after that he abandoned the watermelons and took up selling golf balls, plucked out of the lakes and off the fairways of a nearby country club.

When the boy first started coming to the off ramp, he must have been about eight years old. He used to wear an old football top, too big for him, and a pair of black shorts that almost came down to his knees. Some days he had shoes, some days he didn't. Some days he used to work his way down through the cars queued up at the traffic lights, one after the other, pressing whatever he was selling to the windscreens of the vehicles. Some days, mostly summer days, he'd just stand under the shade of the nearest tree and watch as each car left the highway, a sombre, distant look in the dark of his eyes.

Zill did that same drive for nine years before suddenly – on the morning of 21 May – the boy wasn't at the off ramp. He tried to imagine the reasons why, hoped that it might be because the boy had found something better: a job, a trade, some way to improve himself.

But, eventually, Zill found out that wasn't why the boy never came back.

#Friday_22_June_2007

The railway station was barely that any more. Its platform was eighty feet of crumbling concrete, its corrugated iron roof a punctured, broken shell, its lines bent and rusted orange. The building, its walls and its surrounds were adrift in a sea of grass, nature claiming it back inch by inch. In the fifteen years since a train had last run through, it had become a dumping ground. Rotting food. Plastic. Mulched cereal boxes.

Beer cans. Needles.

People.

Lucinda moved under the crime scene tape and down towards the body, forensic gloves on, camera around her neck. The woman had been left face down on what remained of the tracks, her corpse hidden in the long grass. Cars had been unable to see her through the scrub as they'd passed by on the loneliness of the nearest road, two hundred feet back. Instead she'd been found by two girls from a township half a mile east. They'd been chasing a stray dog with pieces of discarded lead piping.

For a week it had been unseasonably warm for June, the sun beating down out of a clear African sky, and as the ground dipped into a cleft in the earth, and then rose again, the smell hit her: a terrible, cloying stench of decay. Lucinda raised a hand to her mouth.

Familiar faces circled the body: Moses, a wiry forty-year-old Xhosa from Matzikama, on his haunches beside the girl, gloves and mask on, talking to one of the forensic techs; a couple of uniformed officers who she'd got into a routine of talking to in the kitchen in the mornings; and then Ben Zill, off beyond the corpse. He wasn't even looking at the body. Instead, he had his back to the entire crime scene. His gaze was out across the parched yellow scrubland, grass swaying in the breeze, the blue smudge of the city skyline visible in the distance. The crime scene was only five miles from central Cape Town – but it could have been a different planet.

Sometimes this whole country felt like that to Lucinda.

As she got to the body, she stopped. Half-covered by dry grass, the woman's blue floral dress was up around her waist and her buttocks were exposed. Lucinda placed a hand on her camera, working her finger across the casing. Back and forth, back and forth. She realized she'd started doing it more and more in the time she'd been here, automatically, instinctively trying to seek comfort in something she loved. She'd seen some of the cops here, even hardened detectives like Moses, doing the same;

facing down the awfulness of every new crime with something that could anchor them. Moses had a red pen he rolled between his forefinger and thumb. As he stood, glancing at Lucinda, she saw it tucked behind his ear. He backed away and removed it without even thinking.

'Okay, LB.'

She looked at Moses. 'You ready for me?'

He nodded.

They'd shortened her name – Lucinda Berrington – to her initials because it was too long for the lazier cops to say, and too complicated for the ones who weren't confident in English. As she raised the camera to her face, she took a step closer to the woman and saw an evidence marker in the grass off to her right. Beside it lay an old bicycle chain. As she focused in on that, out of the corner of her eye she saw Zill start to move. Snapping a photograph, she dropped the camera to her chest again, watching him return through the grass. When he got to the body he stood there, looking down at the woman, a distant expression on his face. Moses asked him if he needed anything, but Zill just shook his head. Suddenly there was a marked kind of sadness to him.

Most people here sought their sanctuary in something.

A camera. A pen.

Another person.

But not Zill.

Even after more than seven months, Lucinda wasn't sure *what* brought him comfort. In fact, after seven months, she wasn't sure she knew Ben Zill at all.

#Wednesday_27_June_2007

Lucinda watched Zill's car approach, coming along the dusty track towards the place she was staying in. A creaking 1920s bungalow, the only thing she really liked about it was the view from the front veranda, out across Kleinkop, a small town on the edges of the city. During the day, the sun would act like bleach, revealing the town's blemishes: the functionality of its layout; the similarity of its homes; the greyness of its industry. When the night came, everything changed: it became a sea of lights, washing off into the darkness, the constant hum of approaching lorries like a mechanical heartbeat. She'd grown up in Dorset but spent most of her adult life in London, so she found the noise of towns and cities comforting. And yet here, on the hill above Kleinkop, there was a kind of solitude too – a quietness that became even more pronounced at night – that reminded her of her childhood, of running with her sisters across the shingle on Christchurch beach.

Zill pulled up, rousing her from her thoughts, and popped the boot. He didn't get out. She'd discovered pretty quickly that he was never going to win any awards for chivalry. Picking up her camera bags, she hauled them around to the back herself.

'Morning, Ben,' she said as she returned to the front.

'Morning. How are you?'

'Fine. You?'

He nodded. They pulled a U-turn and headed back down the road, a cloud of red dust forming behind them. 'Ready for another day in the corps?'

She smiled. 'I guess I am.'

Lucinda had been in South Africa since the previous November. She'd started out in London as a travel photographer, taking pictures of hotels for holiday brochures. But that had become boring fast, so – at twenty-four – she'd enrolled in a photojournalism course, a decision that had been prompted by dreams of covering important conflicts, of being on the frontline during revolutions. Reality hit a year later: unable to secure commissions from the nationals, and unwilling to settle for work with local papers, her professor – who was from Durban – suggested she apply for a secondment with the South African Police Service that he'd seen advertised in a magazine for ex-pats. SAPS needed a photographer for a year to document the work of their detective teams, as part of a government investigation into whether the department was over-resourced. Two weeks later, she was reporting to Ben Zill. Twenty-four hours after that she was standing on the shore of the Atlantic Ocean close to Cape Point, taking pictures of two dead children.

'How old are you again, LB?' Zill asked her.

She glanced at him. 'Twenty-eight.'

The silence was briefly filled by a pop from the suspension as it hit a pockmark in the road. 'Almost the same age as Jo Vorster.'

That was the name of the victim they'd found at the abandoned station.

Lucinda didn't know what to say.

'I wonder what the killer would have done if that bicycle chain hadn't been lying around?' Zill continued. 'Do you think he would have strangled her with his bare hands?'

'I don't know.'

'You don't have an opinion?'

'I'm just a photographer, Ben.'

He seemed disappointed.

They sat there in silence again, heading down the track towards the junction for the main road. Zill lived on the other side of Kleinkop. When he'd found out – about two months after she started – that she lived three kilometres down the road from him, he'd offered to start picking her up in the mornings.

'You ever heard of Twitter?'

She frowned. 'Twitter?'

'I hear my wife talking about it sometimes. I think she's on it. It's all . . . ' He used a flat palm to show it went over his head. 'Do you use it yourself?'

'I have an account. It's all quite new.'

'What do you do in it?'

'You follow people and they follow you. You ever heard of MySpace, or this new thing, Facebook? It's a bit like that – but, with Twitter, when you're speaking to people, or updating your status, you can only use up to 140 characters.'

'So it's like a short email?'

'Kind of. Why do you ask?'

'We found a bag, discarded in the grass about half a mile west of the body. It was hers. She'd used it to keep her university laptop in. Except the laptop was gone. All that was left inside was the spare battery for it. Anyway, forensics discovered she had a Twitter account. From what I've been told, Twitter's big in the States and Europe, but hasn't really taken off in most of South Africa yet. Except you know where it *has* taken off?'

'No.'

'The universities.'

'So what are you saying?'

'One of her friends, Tara Rowe, sent her a message the night she was last seen. Tara told Jo that all their varsity pals were planning an evening out, and that they were meeting at seven-thirty on Rhodes Memorial Street. You know where that is?'

She did. It was in the foothills of Devil's Peak, part of the range that eventually rolled into Table Mountain.

'Except,' Zill continued, 'Tara Rowe never sent that message.'

Lucinda looked at him. 'What do you mean?'

'Tara was on the other side of the country until yesterday. The message didn't come from the east coast. It came from inside the university, here in Cape Town.'

Lucinda got it instantly. 'So the killer logged in as Tara Rowe?'

Zill nodded.

'Do we know where in the university he logged in?'

'The library.'

'Are there cameras in that part of the building?'

A half-smile. 'Now you're thinking like a cop.'

'*Are* there?'

'No.'

'So basically we've got no idea who *really* sent her that message?'

Zill glanced at her. 'We interviewed eighty-five students who told us they were in and around the library in the days before Jo was murdered, and a few of them said the passwords had been changed on their accounts. Worse, when they went back through their timelines, they found messages to friends they'd never actually sent themselves.'

'The killer sent them.'

'Right. He came into the library, he went through the PCs – probably over the course of two or three days – and, if a student had forgotten to log out of their account properly, he got in, changed their password and started stalking their friends. Some he sent messages to, pretending to be the student in question. But most of his time seems to have been spent trawling accounts and clicking on profile pictures.'

'He was choosing a victim.'

'Right again. Fortunately, most of the students realized someone had gained access to their account, and changed their passwords. But Tara Rowe didn't. She was on the other side of the country at her mother's surprise sixtieth. It was *such* a surprise, Tara didn't tell anyone – so Jo Vorster still thought she was here in Cape Town.'

And went to meet her, Lucinda thought.

'What did the message say?'

Keeping one hand on the wheel, he removed a piece of folded paper from the breast pocket of his shirt and handed it across to her. She took it from him and unfolded it. Printed out was the direct message conversation between Jo Vorster and Tara Rowe.

Except it hadn't been Tara Rowe.

It had been the man who'd raped and killed Jo Vorster.

'The spelling's terrible,' Lucinda said, looking at the printout. The messages were innocuous, but even Jo had commented on her friend's sudden lapse in grammar, joking that she might need to pay more attention in lectures.

In response, the man pretending to be Tara had agreed, made light of it, and asked Jo to confirm that she was definitely going to be at the meeting place on Rhodes Memorial Street.

'What does the spelling tell you?' Zill said.

She looked down at the printout again, her mind ticking over. 'That English isn't his first language.'

'Correct.'

'So the assumption is . . .'

Zill nodded. 'He won't be of British descent. We have fibres from the body and DNA at the scene. That'll tell us his race.'

'That's good.'

'Is it?'

She frowned. 'Well, we have a lead.'

'It's worthless. He used a public space to log into a public computer, so his IP address isn't going to take us anywhere. There are no cameras where we needed them to be. And even if we zero in on his race, how is that going to help? There are twenty thousand students at the university, over four thousand staff. Of the eighty-five students we've already interviewed, *no one* remembers seeing anyone suspicious. We're not talking about some guy who wandered in off the streets here. Her killer blends in. He's smart.'

'Ben, I think – '

'It's a dead end.'

They drove in silence for a while after that, accompanied by the gentle wheeze of the car's suspension as it bounced on the uneven track.

'Is this how you imagined your life turning out?'

She turned to him. 'What do you mean?'

'This. Photographing dead people.'

Abruptly, the atmosphere had changed. He sounded funereal, distressed, troubled. In her time here, she'd noticed that Zill was a man beset by sudden despondency, like he kept reaching the end of the same road.

'I don't know, Ben.'

'You're still young, I guess.'

'You're not *that* old.'

A flicker of a smile on his face.

'Are you okay?' she asked.

'What about her?'

'Who?'

'Jo Vorster.'

His voice had become brittle and quiet.

'What about her?' Lucinda asked.

He didn't reply immediately, eyes fixed on the road ahead. But then, finally, he turned to Lucinda. 'Do you think this is how she imagined her life turning out?'

#Friday_29_June_2007

Looking back, Zill had given his wife a lot of reasons to leave. One time, he forgot to pick their daughter up from the airport after she'd returned from a friend's in Johannesburg. Susan called him in a fit of rage about ninety minutes after April landed, and told him he was a selfish prick. It was hard to argue the point, as he was sitting in a bar at the time. All he ended up doing in the days after was what he'd begun to do a lot: apologize. That was the man he'd become, filling space with weightless words, trying to head her off.

Another time, not long after that, he promised Susan he'd get her car looked at. It had failed to start one morning when she was leaving for work and she'd had to call in an emergency day's holiday because he was on the other side of the city with his phone turned off. They'd always had problems with the car. Little, niggly things: ticking in the engine, rattly windows, flat batteries. He'd take it down to a guy he knew in the city, the guy would tweak one thing on it, then a couple of weeks later something else would go. When he got home on that Tuesday night – a week after they found Jo Vorster – he discovered the car had sprung an oil leak.

'This is ridiculous, Ben,' Susan said to him.

'I'm sorry.'

'We need a new car.'

He'd had a bad day – another long, dark, fruitless day stalking the shadows for Vorster's faceless killer – and didn't much feel like discussing it, so he fobbed her off, told her to leave it with him, and disappeared into the bedroom. He was tired, bone tired, but in the hush of the room, under the purr of the fan, he felt an unexpected peace take hold: a rare moment of stillness, every terrible moment from another terrible day washing out into the corners of the room. He hadn't slept well for months. Sometimes, when he lay there in the darkness in the middle of the night, he wondered if he ever would again.

But then Susan came in. Her face was twisted and angry. 'So you want me to leave the car for you to sort out – is that right?'

He didn't reply.

'That's just the problem, though, Ben, isn't it?'

He sat up and swung his legs around. 'Look, Suze –'

'Were you even aware we had a damp problem in the kitchen?'

He looked at her.

'*Were* you? Because *I* was the one who called the guy about it. *I* was the one who waited in for him. *I* was the one who got it fixed.'

'I'm sorry.'

'I don't want an *apology*, Ben.'

He watched as her face filled with colour, blooming in her cheeks like pools of blood. This time, trying to take the sting out of the conversation, he said nothing.

But she wasn't finished.

'I told you about the damp problem twice – and you *still* didn't do anything about it. I'm not even sure it registers with you when I speak. It's like I'm talking to a ghost.'

'I'm sorry, okay?'

'*Stop telling me you're sorry!*'

She paused, breath ragged, standing over him at the edge of the bed, one hand on the dresser next to her, the other on her hip. She looked old for a moment, beaten down, which was rare for her. They were both in their forties, but she'd always looked better on it: he saw himself in the mirror sometimes and got scared by the man who looked back. Pale, almost grey, like a refraction of the person in the photo frames on their walls.

'I can't talk about this now,' he said.

'Why not?'

'If you knew what kind of shit I'd had to deal with today . . .'

'That's *every day of our lives*, Ben. *Every* day.'

'What do you want me to say?'

'Anything.'

'What the hell does that mean?'

'Say anything to me, Ben. Anything. Anything that isn't to do with your work. Anything that isn't an excuse as to why you're late, or why you forgot to pick your daughter up. Because you know what I get out of you the rest of the time? Nothing.'

He felt himself tense. 'You don't understand.'

'What don't I understand, Ben?'

For some reason, he thought of Lucinda Berrington, and something he'd said to her: *Is this how you imagined your life turning out?*

He shrugged. 'I'm trying to pay the bloody bond on our house, keep the water and lights running, our medical, our pension. When I'm not doing that, I'm standing at a disused railway station next to a girl who's been raped, who's been strangled to death with a bicycle chain, and thinking: "What the fuck is wrong with the world?"'

'Oh, not this shit again.'

'Yes, this shit again.'

He got up from the bed.

'It's your job, Ben. It's been your job for twenty-five years.'

'And, in twenty-five years, you've never understood.'

It was a cheap shot, and they both knew it.

He stepped past her but she came up behind him and grabbed his arm. 'Do you even remember your daughter growing up?'

He turned to face her – prickling with anger, light-headed with exhaustion – looking at her hand on his arm. 'What the hell kind of a question is that?'

'I listened to you a couple of weeks ago – when you actually made the effort to get home and sit down with us for dinner – and you were remembering things that never even happened. Do you know that? Do you even *realize* what you're saying? You've invented a version of her childhood: things you did with her, places you took her. But you never did any of those things with her, Ben. April's sixteen and you've never been here.'

He studied her. 'That's bullshit.'

'It's not bullshit. This picture-perfect memory you have of her growing up, it doesn't exist. You're rewriting history based on what you *wanted* it to be like.'

'No,' he said.

'Yes, Ben.'

'No.' *That's a lie. She's lying. I'm not remembering things wrong. I'm not losing my grip. I'm tired, but I'm not losing my grip.* He shrugged her off. 'Leave me alone.'

She grabbed him again.

He shrugged her off a second time. 'Leave me *alone*!'

And then it happened so fast, it was done before he could stop himself: she went to grab him again and he pushed her away, hand flat to the centre of her chest. She stumbled back, hitting the corner of the bed – and, as she did, it knocked her off-balance, and she pirouetted and fell face-first into the dresser.

Shit.

Oh shit.

He rushed across the room towards her. She'd fallen beyond the bed, hidden from him, her legs visible but nothing else. When she saw him coming, she scrambled on to all fours and scurried away, into the corner of the room, backing up against the wall. There was blood running down her face.

'No,' he said. 'No, no, no. I'm so sorr –'

'Get away from me, Ben.'

'Please,' he said, dropping to his knees in front of her. 'Please forgive me.'

'I . . . ' There were tears in her eyes now. 'I don't know who you are any more.'

He held out a hand to her. 'Please, Suze.'

'Who are you, Ben?'

'Please . . . ' Tears filled his own eyes now. 'I'm your husband.'

#Friday_3_August_2007

The second woman was found dead on the third of August. She lived in a place called Bristol, a mid-sized town on the other side of Kleinkop. At night, if the evening was clear, Lucinda could sometimes see Bristol from the veranda of her house, its series of gridded streets tracing the blackness of the Atlantic Ocean.

She was late arriving, having been photographing cadets at the academy, and by the time she got to the house, everyone was already there, gathered around the body. The victim was older than Vorster, but had been treated by the murderer with as little respect. She'd been punched in the throat, and had fallen through a glass coffee table in the middle of the living room. As she laid there, dazed, her attacker had raped her, strangled her with a tie that had been left on a chair in the kitchen, and then vanished. On a second sweep of the house, Moses discovered that the killer not only appeared to have taken money from the bedroom, but had also raided the victim's jewellery box.

'You think he took something as a trophy?' Lucinda overheard one of the uniformed officers asking Moses. Lucinda looked to Zill, who barely reacted, and then to Moses, a man who rarely offered an opinion unless he knew it to be right.

Moses left the room.

On a drive into work during her first three months with SAPS, back when Zill didn't so readily let his guard down in front of her, he'd told Lucinda he'd once been an expert spotter of talent. 'But then people stopped wanting to be cops,' he'd said, 'so I've been reduced to recruiting second-rate cadets just to fill spaces.' But he'd always spoken highly of Moses. 'He's from a different time,' Zill had said.

'Was it a better time too?'

'In some ways.'

Yet, as she watched Zill standing in the carnage of the living room, eyes on the woman, on the bed of shattered glass she was lying on, Lucinda wondered whether there had ever been, or ever would be, a better time. In the old days, South Africa had a racist government storming townships, massacring innocent people as they scattered through the scorched streets. Now they just had this: an enemy with no cause at all.

'Do you?' Zill said.

They all looked around. Zill was staring past Lucinda, almost through her, to the uniformed officer.

'Do I what, sir?' the officer replied.

'Do you think he took something as a trophy?'

She glanced at Lucinda. 'I, uh . . . '

Lucinda looked from Zill to the officer and back to Zill, his face chalk-white, days of stubble lining his jowls. 'Ben, do you want me to start taking photographs?'

He just looked at her.

'Ben?'

No reply.

Lucinda looked around the room. Without Moses, there was no one willing to step in. No ranking officer. No deputy for Zill. A couple of the forensic techs glanced at her, their thoughts projected onto their faces: *Ask him what the hell he wants us to do.* There was a sudden kind of panic in the room, something heavy and unspoken. Lucinda felt like she was on the outside, looking in. What did they all know that she didn't?

She looked from face to face.

No one helped her.

So she turned back to Ben: 'Ben, what do you want us –'

'Everyone out,' Zill said.

'Do you want me to –'

'I don't want anything from you,' he said to her, quietly, evenly, without a hint of emotion. Then he looked around the room. 'I don't want anything from *any* of you.'

As she stood with the others on the outside of the murder room, she found out what was going on. To start with, in the moments after she'd first arrived, she'd thought it had been because Zill was first on the scene. She'd come to realize that a lot of cops felt an attachment to the case when that happened, as if it was theirs by default.

Then she thought it was the location: the fact that it had twenty-four-hour security and two fenced gates, two guards at the first, and yet the killer had got beyond both – and back out again – without anyone appearing to notice.

But it wasn't those things.

Zill saw the connection to Jo Vorster the instant he arrived at the scene. Both had been strangled. Both had been raped. Both had been left face down, dresses around their waists, discarded like they meant nothing. There were twenty years between the two victims, but physically they were almost the same: blonde, fair skinned, slim. The only difference was that Vorster had been dumped miles from her family home, while the second woman had died inside hers, the killer presumably deciding that it was too risky to get a body out of what was – in name, at least – a secure complex.

Yet he'd opted for the same method to trap both victims, this time using Vorster's laptop and another UCT student's Twitter account to send direct messages to the victim.

'She seems too old to be a student,' Lucinda said to Moses.

Moses looked at her. 'That's because she's not. We found a DM in her Twitter account, sent yesterday from a student who's out of the country this week. It's just like we thought: the killer's stealing identities and posing as UCT students. *He's* not a student. He just pretends he belongs there. The woman thought the person turning up today was called Cebo Bhongela. She phoned down to the guards at the front of the complex here and told them to wave him through. So the guy turns up, tells the guards he's Bonghela, and they wave him through.'

'Did the guards get a look at him?'

'We've got a physical description.'

'Anything we can use?'

Moses shrugged. 'No identifying marks. Average height. Average weight. There are one-point-three million black Africans in this city. You do the maths.'

DNA from the Jo Vorster murder had already confirmed that the killer was black, so the name of Cebo Bonghela would fit just fine. As long as he didn't do anything to get himself noticed on the way in or the way out, he could pass through without raising as much as an eyebrow. Lucinda felt a fizz of frustration, for Moses, for Zill, for Jo Vorster, for the woman lying dead on the floor of the living room. But when she looked back at Moses, she saw something else in his face. Not just frustration.

Sadness.

'What's going on, Moses?' she asked.

He looked at her. Swallowed. 'The woman in there didn't know Bonghela was out of the country. Instead, she thought he was coming here to discuss his dissertation.'

'Wait, so the victim's a lecturer?'

After she'd asked the question, the hallway hushed, every face slowly turning in her direction. 'Yes,' Moses said softly.

'Do we know her name?'

'Yes,' he said again. 'Her name is Susan Zill.'

#Monday_6_August_2007

In the month after he'd pushed her against the dresser, he'd tried to make it up to Susan by taking care of the jobs that needed doing. One of them was getting the car fixed. He took it to the normal place, the guy replaced something, and then Zill brought it back home and assured her everything would be fine. And, for thirty-five days, it was.

But then the car stopped working again.

On 3 August, the morning she was killed, it had been her day off. Susan had wanted to go to the mall at Century City, and ordinarily he would have just loaned her his car and organized a lift with someone else, but he needed to pick Lucinda up and then drive them both down to the station where there was a press conference for the Jo Vorster case. 'I'm so sorry, Suze,' he'd said to her. 'If it was any other day, you could have just had my car.'

'It's fine.'

'I'm really sorry.'

'It's *fine*, Ben.'

That was how conversations had gone since the incident: him apologizing, her telling him it was fine, even though clearly, understandably, it wasn't. The irony was, he actually meant every word in those last days of her life. His apologies were no longer weightless. He'd only have to look at her before he began immediately telling her he was sorry. He began wondering whether it might have been easier – for both of them, though more selfishly for him – if she'd just upped and left. But she didn't, perhaps because of April.

Perhaps, even more understandably, to punish him.

'You want a hand with that?'

As he'd been trying to get Susan's Polo started that morning, Zill had looked across the road to the houses opposite. The day she'd died had been a cold, wet morning marked by granite skies, and one of his neighbours, a podgy man in his fifties called du Toit, had been standing out front in shorts, a shirt and a raincoat. In his hand he held a video camera. Beyond him, visible through one of the windows of his house, Zill had glimpsed du Toit's wife, Patricia, stick-thin and greying. They'd only been in there a month, but Zill had never taken to her. He'd never really taken to either of them.

Despite that, Zill had smiled politely. 'I'm fine.'

'Sounds like you've got a bit of a problem there.'

'Sounds like it.'

Du Toit must have seen Zill's eyes move to the camera. He'd smiled, and held it up. 'Nothing sinister,' he said. 'Used to work as a cameraman for SABC until they kicked me out for being too white.' He'd rolled his eyes, as if expecting to find some solidarity in Zill's face. Zill just nodded. 'Anyway,' he said, 'just trying to keep my eye in.'

A couple of minutes later, after du Toit had disappeared back inside, and the rain had started to get harder, Zill had given up on the Polo.

Two hours later, his wife was dead.

In the early hours of 6 August he began to dream of a different outcome; of the moment he got the car started and Susan headed out in her Polo to the mall. And when he woke up from the dream that morning and peeled back the sweat-stained sheets, he sat looking out at the rain, imagining other scenarios too: leaving home, forgetting something and then coming back and finding the killer already in his house. Zill began to fantasize about what he would do to him: imagined his knuckles pounding down into the killer's face, chest, stomach, over and over until all Zill could see was blood. He imagined the sound those strikes would make – *thud, thud, thud* – and the wet, choking gargle coming from deep in the killer's throat. But mostly he imagined leaving him lying there, dazed, casually walking through to the bedroom, selecting one of his ties, and returning to the living room. He imagined knotting it around the killer's neck, just like the killer had knotted it around Susan's. He imagined strangling him.

He imagined seeing the light go out.

Instead, as he got ready for work, Zill's mind returned to what really happened: forty minutes after trying to get the car started, he gave up. 'I'm probably going to be late tonight because we've got a stats meeting,' he'd said to Susan after that. 'Plus I'm going to pop into Motor City on the way home and see if we can't replace this piece of crap.'

She'd maybe smiled then.

He hoped she had, just like he hoped he'd kissed her and told her he loved her, but the truth was, in the three days since she'd been gone, he had no clear idea of whether he did or didn't. He was forty minutes late by then, and though he'd tried not to let his anxiety play out on his face, his mind was already in the office, in the files that awaited him, in the crime scenes he was yet to walk. He couldn't even recall if he'd waved to her, or spent a moment looking back. Normally she stood on the steps at the side of their house as he left. Normally he waved back, one hand out the window as he moved through the security gates at the front of the complex. But that day was a blank.

Perhaps he did wave. Perhaps he didn't.

He liked to think he did.

Even if, deep down, he feared he'd forgotten.

#Wednesday_12_September_2007

Cape Town Central Station sits in the shadow of Table Mountain, an ugly red-brick building that looks more like a prison. Before he ran Murder and Robbery, Zill had told Lucinda that he'd worked a lot of gang crime, carving out a niche for himself on the third floor of the station. On their way into work in the mornings, he'd drive along Baden-Powell, a beautiful, desolate coastal road that wound its way east towards Khayelitsha, Cape Town's biggest township, and he'd give her a running commentary of the things he'd seen. But after Susan was killed, the commentaries stopped. After Susan was killed, they rarely spoke in the mornings. Lucinda became so uncomfortable with it that, without even realizing, she started bringing her camera bag into the front with her. She'd sit it on her lap, let her fingers move up and down the plastic casing, finding comfort in it, and watch Khayelitsha pass in a blur. Occasionally Zill would ask her something, small, inane things, perhaps about her year's contract almost being at an end, but often they'd drive for an hour in silence. And, in the silence, she became more and more aware of her surroundings.

Most days, even ten months in, she'd still be surprised at the size of Khayelitsha, a vast, sprawling satellite town built on about a millionth of the budget of the rest of the city. Shacks mixed with whitewashed one-room houses; garbage blew along the streets; there was no drainage, few street lights. Zill had once told her that its people were either proud, always looking for an exit and a way to better themselves, or they were fighting against their circumstances, trying to hit out. 'That's how gangs are made,' he used to tell her. 'Anger, resentment, desperation building and bubbling away.'

That was what Zill had dealt with for seven years, what he faced down – and what some people in the police service believed had come back to bite him.

'He made enemies in Khayelitsha,' she heard an Afrikaans cop say one morning in the first week. 'The gangs there, they remember him. The crews, the leaders, they *hate* him. He shut them down. He took their weapons. He confiscated their drugs.'

And so the whispers began, in the corridors of the station, out in the bars after work and then finally in the newspapers. Even though it was clear he was targeting victims through Twitter, some said the killer was a member of a gang Zill had shut down. Others, that Jo Vorster had actually been a practice run for the ultimate act of revenge.

Susan Zill.

Lucinda would stand there, camera around her neck, awaiting instructions from whoever was supposed to be in charge, listening to rumours being spread. Zill was always retreating to his office and pulling the blinds; Moses – stubbled, eyes a buttery yellow – seemed unsure how to make the step up. Lucinda heard him on the phone to his wife one day, talking in Xhosa, and although she didn't understand, she got the gist: *How do I tell Zill to step back from the murder of his own wife?* It shouldn't have been his job, it should have been the job of Zill's boss, whoever that was. Someone should have stepped in. But the reality was there was no one else senior enough to give the case to.

'When I took over Murder and Robbery,' Zill had told her once, right back at the start, 'I ended up with a few old white men harbouring secrets they would never give voice to, and a barrage of young black men, idealistic and passionate, but unworldly and untrained. This place is a mess. A mess of personalities, of cultures, of politics. It's understaffed and under-resourced. I've attended twenty police funerals in the last year. I have a whiteboard in my office, where I construct a checklist of active cases. There are so many, I've had to stick pieces of paper to the wall beside the board, and start a separate, handwritten list.'

But, even though he shut himself away with his whiteboard and his wall of paper, Zill wasn't immune to the rumours either. One evening, when they were returning along Baden-Powell, Khayelitsha rolling off into the darkness of another winter night, he said to her: 'Do you believe what they're saying?'

Lucinda had turned to him.

It was the first thing he'd said in days.

'What who are saying?'

'I overhear them in the station.' His voice was cracked, and he smelled of cigarette smoke. He'd got into the car that morning stinking of booze too.

'People will always talk, Ben.'

'Do you think that's what happened?'

'What?'

'That I got her killed.'

'You didn't get her killed.'

'I got her killed if it was a gang that did it.'

She didn't know what to say, so said nothing.

Yet, as the days went on, Lucinda became more and more involved in the case. Zill seemed not to trust anyone else, and refused to engage with officers he thought had been talking about him behind his back. When Moses went down with pneumonia, Zill began using Lucinda as his sounding board. He was worn and broken, but he was at least conscious of how it would look asking a photographer on secondment for her opinion on a double murder – so he kept their chats confined to the drive into, and back from, work. Inside a month, she knew the case inside out.

She knew that there were no CCTV cameras in the Zill's housing complex, so Ben had to rely on eyewitnesses. She knew the front gates of the complex opened up on to a road with no shops on it and no other houses, so an appeal in the newspaper brought forward men and women who believed they were passing at the time the killer entered or left, or sometimes both. She knew it led nowhere. The witnesses were well-intentioned but inexact, they were confused, or they were fantasists. Zill told Lucinda that Susan had chosen the house for its location:

unspoilt, surrounded by forests, with a glimpse of the sea. But its proximity to vast, uncontrolled bush, its location away from the city's main arteries, made it porous and, worse, it made it lonely. The thing they'd loved about it, the *reason* they'd chosen the complex in the first place, was the weakness that exposed it.

Lucinda even went with Zill to interview the guards – two kids who had both failed police entrance exams – and realized it wouldn't have taken much to outwit them. When one of them said he always took a cigarette break in the forest beyond the walls of the complex – because his employers banned him from smoking at the front gates – she could see 3 August playing out in front of them: the killer sat and watched the routine of the guards, and then, when one of them went out for a smoke, he made his approach, telling the remaining guard that he was Susan's student, Cebo Bonghela. Zill asked – basically pleaded – with the guard for a better physical description, but he gave him little. Lucinda told Zill that she thought the Twitter lead would dry up too: the killer wasn't going to draw anyone else in that way – at least not for a while. He was too careful; too calculating. Zill said they'd have to wait and see.

But she knew he thought the same.

Then, a month later, the weather began to change. The ridges of the city emerged from the mist, cloud gave way to sky, rain to sun – and, at 9 p.m., on the evening of 12 September, Lucinda received a phone call.

'You're the journalist, right?' a male voice asked her.

He was English.

'Photographer,' Lucinda corrected him. 'Who is this?'

'People tell me you've got Zill's ear.'

'I don't know about that.'

'Do you or don't you?'

She looked across the office. Zill's door was open and he was sitting in front of the whiteboard, looking at the crime scene photographs from the two murders. Next to his PC, he'd disconnected his phone, its wire snaking off the edge of the desk.

'Yes,' she said finally.

'You have his ear?'

'Yes.'

'Then tell him he needs to meet me tomorrow.'

'Who is this?'

'My name's David Raker,' the caller said. 'I think I can help him.'

#Thursday_13_September_2007

They met in a café on Loop Street. Raker was an Englishman in his early thirties, tall and broad, dark haired and handsome, despite a week's beard growth. He already had a pen and pad adjacent to one another on the table in front of him. The pen had the name of his newspaper written on it. As Zill approached, Raker got up and the two of them shook hands. There was a brief moment of discomfort – a silence as they both sized each other up – and then the waitress wandered over and took their order. Zill ordered a cheeseburger and a bottle of Castle; Raker a black coffee and a chicken salad.

'I was sorry to hear about your wife,' Raker said.

Zill eyed him and then nodded, shrugging off the jacket he'd been wearing. 'You don't sound like a local.'

'I'm just passing through.'

'Doing what?'

'I was here for the elections in 1994. I came back in 2000 to write a story on the country, to see what had changed. They've asked me to do the same this year.'

'And after that?'

'I'm flying out to Los Angeles next week to cover the elections.'

Zill looked at the cars passing on Loop Street, sun glinting off their windows. A line of palm trees bisected the road, fronds gently snapping and twisting in the breeze.

'Where's your colleague?' Raker asked.

Zill pointed further up the street, to where Lucinda was waiting in the passenger seat of his Audi. 'You said you wanted to meet me alone.'

'I'll tell you what I know,' Raker said, 'then you can decide yourself whether you want to share it with her. I don't know what kind of arrangement you have with her.'

'What's that supposed to mean?'

Raker held up a hand. 'Nothing. Calm down.'

'What do you want, Raker?'

'It's about your wife.'

Zill felt himself stiffen. 'What about her?'

The waitress re-emerged with their drinks. Raker leaned back in his seat, pulling his pad towards him. 'Is there anything else I can get you?' she asked them.

Raker was the only one to reply: 'That's fine. Thank you.'

As soon as the waitress was out of earshot, Zill edged

forward in his seat, arms out in front of him, hands flat to the table. 'What about my wife?'

'Do you know a Patricia du Toit?'

Zill frowned. 'She lives in the same housing complex as me. So?'

'So she works for one of my newspaper's affiliates here in Cape Town, as a PA. They rent space in our office. Anyway, I've got to know her a little bit and – a month or so back – she told me her husband was currently out of work. Do you know him too?'

Zill thought of the last time he'd seen the husband. *The morning Susan was killed.* Du Toit had been carrying a video camera, watching Zill try to get the Polo started.

'Zill?' Raker said. 'Do you know him too?'

'Not really.'

Raker flipped open the front page of his pad. It was full of notes. When Zill tried to decipher some of it, he realized it was all in shorthand. 'Her husband's called Andre. Patricia told me that he's spent the last six months out of work since he was given the boot by SABC. She said he's been unable to find anything else in TV, so – in order to help pay the bills – he's started doing a few odd jobs in and around the complex: repairing things, fixing them, making sure the place is all up together.' Raker paused. Zill watched him read on through his notes – before finally looking up. 'It means he's always around. And he was home the day your wife was killed.'

Zill tilted his head. '*And?*'

Raker shifted in his seat. He suddenly looked hesitant, as if something had disturbed him. 'Look, for what it's worth, I don't call this journalism.'

'What the hell are you talking about?'

Raker took a deep breath. 'When the story about your wife hit, the editor of our affiliate found out Patricia knew you. Well, knew you as a neighbour. So he started chatting to her. Before long, it became clear that she was prepared to talk about you, to talk about you both. So was her husband. They're struggling to pay the mortgage. They saw an opportunity to make some money, the editor here saw a story. Especially as . . . the du Toit's were prepared to embellish things.'

'Embellish things?'

Raker eyed Zill. 'Apparently there were some rumours about you and your wife having an argument, about . . . ' He paused. 'About you possibly hitting her.'

Zill grabbed Raker by the collar and pulled him across the table. Raker instantly hit back, ripping Zill's hand away and shoving him back into his seat. Zill, teeth clenched, anger burning a hole in his chest, came forward again. 'Are you kidding me? You're actually trying to *blackmail* me, you fucking asshole?'

Raker shook his head. 'Listen to me.'

'I will have you arrest—'

'*Listen* to me,' Raker said, and the two of them realized the people at the tables nearest to them had all turned to watch. Raker waited for the attention to die down. 'Try to listen to what I'm telling you. The paper wants to write a story about you being a wife-beater. One of their guys cornered your daughter in a shopping mall a few weeks back and tricked her into talking about you. They've got some quotes about you misremembering her childhood. You sound like you're losing your grip, Ben.'

Zill felt a flutter of panic. 'This can't happen,' he said.

Raker nodded again. Then he reached down to a bag at his feet and removed something. It was a DV tape for a video camera.

'The du Toit's are like everyone else,' he said. 'They think your wife died in some kind of gang hit. They're scared about reprisals and, because they're scared, they can be manipulated. The editor here knows it, I know it, you know it.' He waved the DV tape at Zill. 'The du Toit's have been sitting on this footage for a month. They don't trust the police to keep them safe, which is why they haven't called it in. So, when my editor found out about this tape, he managed to persuade them to keep it back from the cops. He has some fanciful idea about the paper IDing the guy first.'

Zill shook his head.

'Except the only thing that's helping you at the moment is that they haven't been able to find out who the killer is,' Raker said. 'They're still searching. But the paper is *determined* to solve the case and put it on the front page of the local edition. They want to bring this guy in themselves. But what they *really* want to do is take a shot at the government and the police at the same time. SAPS is under-funded, it's corrupt, it's incapable of solving crimes. The same goes for the crooks sitting in parliament up in Pretoria. Can you imagine how much of an embarrassment it would be to them, and to you, if the *media* solved this crime?'

Zill frowned. 'I don't . . . '

'You're the face of failure, Ben. You're the poster child for SAPS. A violent washout who – in their eyes – is as culpable as the man who killed your wife. It's just a matter of time before they ID him. And, when they do, you're done.' Raker placed the tape down between them. 'However, without this, it's your word against theirs.'

Zill looked from the tape to Raker.

'Take this footage,' Raker said. 'Use it. Then burn it.'

He pushed the tape across the table just as their food arrived. Zill took it and set it down beside him. 'Why are you doing this?'

Raker zipped up his bag and shuffled out, flipping open his wallet. He took out a two hundred rand note, placing it down between them.

'I don't know if you hit her or not,' Raker said. 'I hope not. I really do. But, before I came down here today, I called a couple of cops I know at the station – sources I got my claws into the last time I was out here – and asked around about you, and they told me this is the only case you care about. So, whatever it is that's firing you – whether it's love, or guilt, or self-loathing – we both know there's a bigger win here: your wife, and Jo Vorster. Honestly, Ben? I don't give a shit about you. But I sure as hell give a shit about two innocent women. And if I can do something about it, I will.' Raker paused, looking around him and then back at Zill. 'Whatever you decide to do for Susan, however far you decide to take it, know that I would do the same for my wife. Absolutely, without thinking. But don't ever talk about me to anyone. Don't ever call me. Not now, not ever.'

Raker slung his bag over his shoulder.

'As far as you're concerned, we never met.'

And then he headed out into the sun.

#Thursday_13_September_2007

The footage on the tape began in a different time at a different place. Andre du Toit was filming his wife and kids at Noordhoek beach, following the three of them as they chased each other, white sand kicking up behind them, the sun falling behind the ridges of Chapman's Peak. They were dressed in winter coats and in the corner was a time stamp: 29/06/07.

After two and a half minutes, the footage snapped between scenes: from the wide open spaces of the beach at dusk to night inside the housing complex. Du Toit was at his kitchen window, across the road from Zill's house. 'Pat,' du Toit said in Afrikaans, the camera struggling to focus in the lack of light. 'Come here. They're at it again. It's a bad one tonight. Come.' In the brief silence that followed, the camera picked up voices.

Zill and Susan.

It was the night of the argument.

'What do you need that for?' Patricia du Toit said, referring to the camera.

Her husband didn't reply, and soon their attentions were diverted by what was going on at the house across the road, the argument getting louder, carrying out into the cool winter night, snatches of sentences instantly frozen for the camera to hear: *Stop telling me you're sorry! I'm trying to pay the bloody bond on our house! Do you even remember your daughter growing up? That's bullshit!* And then finally silence – until, four minutes later, the kitchen light came on and Susan appeared at the window.

Zill was following her.

He was apologizing.

Susan had blood on her face.

'That bloody bastard,' Patricia du Toit said, as her husband concentrated on zooming as close to the kitchen window as he could get. Suddenly the footage got unsteady and confusing to watch, but it didn't stop the slow march of dread building in Zill's stomach: by the time Andre du Toit zoomed out again, neither Zill nor Susan were in the kitchen. A couple of seconds after that, the film ended.

A crackle.

A snowfall of static.

Zill turned to look at Lucinda. She was sitting behind him in his office, the blinds closed, the door shut. 'It's not what it . . . '

He stopped himself. *It's exactly what it looks like.*

'What the hell did you do, Ben?'

'It was an accident.'

'She had blood on her face.'

'I know.'

'She had *blood* on her face, Ben.'

'I'm sorry,' he said quietly, but he wasn't sure who he was apologizing to any more: Susan, Jo Vorster, Lucinda – in a way, he'd failed them all.

The footage started again.

Du Toit was in the same position at the kitchen sink, lens fixed on the front of Zill's house. In the corner of the screen was another date stamp: 03/08/07.

The day Susan was murdered.

Right at the edge of the shot, a man in his late twenties was coming down the road, dressed smartly in a suit. He came deeper into the complex, head facing away from the camera, looking around him. *He was checking to see if he was being watched.* He walked from right to left – and then, finally, disappeared from the shot.

Cut to black.

The footage kicked in again. Still 3 August. Du Toit still in the same place. Except now he was beginning a slow zoom towards the front door of Zill's house.

It was open.

All Zill could see was the darkness inside; a huge mouth, black and ominous. He heard Lucinda's chair whine gently behind him as she shifted position, and then she came forward, closer to the screen. As Zill sat there in the silence of his office, the darkness of that doorway felt like it was swallowing him up.

A crackle in the microphone as du Toit shifted slightly to his left. A brief burst of noise from his kids in another room. A car somewhere. On the counter, two minutes passed. Then three. Another crackle in the microphone, this time louder, disguising the noise from the children, from the car. Then a long, mournful stillness settled across the complex. Even the kids stopped making noise. As Zill watched, he could feel his hands digging into the seat; his toes curling inside his shoes; his heart pounding against his chest. Lucinda glanced at him, her face pale, a flash of fear in her eyes now too.

They knew what was coming next.

The man emerged from the house. He looked vaguely like the description they'd got from the guards – but not close enough.

Zill heard du Toit draw a long breath and on screen the

image dropped slightly, as he tried to hide himself behind the ridge of the kitchen counter. In the doorway to Zill's house, the man looked around him, checking to see if he was being watched. He wiped the back of his hand on the tail of his shirt; a tiny smear of blood just visible. Then he tucked it in, made sure his trousers were done up, and scanned his surroundings a second time. He paused for a moment on the window of du Toit's house.

Du Toit dropped to the floor.

The microphone cracked against something.

For twenty seconds, all Zill could hear was du Toit's breathing. There was no footage, just sound. The lens was pressing against a trouser leg, the material moving in and out of focus as the lens failed to centre. Eventually du Toit started to get to his knees again, to his feet, bringing the camera up with him and directing it out through their kitchen window. The man was leaving, heading out the other way, his back to the camera, suit jacket back on.

Coiled around the killer's hand was a black necklace.

Susan's necklace.

Hanging from it was a crucifix.

#Monday_29_October_2007

Lucinda tried to help Zill identify the man, but he was a ghost. He wasn't a student. He wasn't a UCT employee. He had no history. She watched and rewatched the footage, over and over again, and got nowhere. The process went on for weeks, through the rest of September and into October, until she knew every second of the tape.

Every day, she would pick up the newspapers and expect to see Zill splashed across the front page, but the story never arrived: Raker had taken the original – presumably deleted any copies that had been made too – and, without the tape, there was no footage of Susan's bloodied face, and no footage of her killer. Zill had been saved from one fate – but not another.

With no tape, there was no story; but with his possession of it, there was no case. He was boxed in. Zill couldn't use the footage to progress a prosecution because he'd obtained it illegally.

He couldn't put the guy's face on a poster.

Instead, she realized, a different fate had befallen him: having to watch his wife's killer repeatedly exit the sanctity of their home, a trace of her blood on his shirt, her necklace in his hand, her crucifix against his fingers. Lucinda imagined what came before was worse still: seeing her alive, breathing as she once did, moving from the hallway and into their kitchen, the evidence of what he'd done to her burned on to the tape forever.

A woman he'd loved, but maybe not enough.

At least, until she was gone.

#Tuesday_6_November_2007

The interview rooms in the Central Station backed on to the kitchen area. One morning, six days after Lucinda left South Africa, Zill looked up from the coffee machine and saw two officers bringing a teenager in. They walked either side of him, a hand on each arm.

It was the boy from the off ramp.

'Hey,' Zill said to them in Afrikaans. 'Hey, stop.'

The officers stopped, eyes flicking between Zill and the boy. 'Is there a problem, sir?' one of them asked politely.

Zill didn't reply, keeping his gaze on the boy. 'You remember me?'

Slowly, the boy looked up. He had a bloodshot eye, a cut on his left cheek and a gaunt, lifeless expression.

'You don't remember me?' Zill said.

The boy shook his head.

Zill glanced at the officers and could see in their faces that they were wondering whether he'd finally flipped. The guy who'd lost his wife, and maybe his mind too. The obsessive who'd never talked to anyone about the case – except for a photographer who was now six thousand miles away.

Eventually, Zill looked at the cops. 'What did he do?'

'We caught him trying to steal a car.'

Zill nodded. 'Give me two minutes with him, okay?'

'Sir, I –'

'Two minutes,' Zill said.

The officers nodded and disappeared back to their desks.

'I passed you every day for nine years at De Waal,' Zill said to the boy.

The boy's eyes narrowed.

'You don't remember?'

He shook his head for a third time.

Zill felt strangely disappointed. He'd always been courteous to the kid; always acknowledged him, even if he hadn't bought his golf balls or his flower pots. Now the boy was staring straight through Zill – just like everyone else had since 3 August.

'Come with me.'

He led the boy along past the kitchen to one of the interview rooms further down and, once inside, directed him to a chair. Zill waited for the door to close.

'Why are you stealing cars?'

The boy finally looked up. 'Why not?'

'What changed?'

'What do you mean?'

'Why did you stop coming to the off ramp?'

The boy stared down into his lap again, to trousers that were coming apart at the seams, to the frayed ends of a Kaiser Chiefs t-shirt. When he finally looked up again, there were tears in his eyes.

'It's okay,' Zill said gently.

'I have no family now,' the boy replied.

'Why?'

'My mother . . . she died this morning.'

Zill paused. 'I'm sorry. Where's your father?'

'Dead.'

'Grandparents?'

He shook his head and wiped some tears away.

'How long have you been stealing cars?' Zill asked.

More tears glistened in his eyes. 'I've been trying to save some money,' he said. 'I've been stealing the cars and selling them to a guy I know in Mitchells Plain. The one I stole this morning . . . I wanted it to be my last. I was going to drive along the coast to Port Elizabeth. I was going to try and start again.'

'What is there in PE for you?'

'Something better than here,' the boy said. 'The disease, it has taken my mother, my father, my grandma. Maybe, eventually, it will take me and my brother. But I'm not going to wait around to find out.'

'Where's your brother?'

He looked at Zill, but said nothing.

'Can't you stay with him?'

'No.'

'Why not?'

He glanced at Zill, as if unsure. Then, he reached into his pocket and took something out.

'He's not someone I can believe in any more,' the boy said.

'What do you mean?'

He showed Zill what he was holding.

It was a black necklace with a crucifix on it.

#*Wednesday_7_November_2007*

The brother lived in a one-room house in a suburb of Khayelitsha called Rocklands. Zill left his car out on Baden-Powell and approached in darkness. The house was on the edge of the development and when Zill found it, he stopped and pulled on a balaclava. Every inch of surrounding scrubland was littered with rotting food and rusting tin cans. On the opposite side of the house he found a window: inside, his wife's killer sat on his own in the corner of the room. He was listening to the radio and laughing.

He looked high.

The room – his bed laid out beside him, a small kitchenette on the far side with dishes in the sink, no carpets, no paint on the walls – was lit by a single candle. On a stool in the corner of the room was a laptop. *Jo Vorster's*. Zill felt a stir of anger.

But then it got worse.

Above the stool was a peg rack with a coverall for a gardening service hanging from it; then the uniform of a local Pick N Pay supermarket; then a shirt, tie and name badge from McDonalds. Next to that, the whites of a hospital porter.

Next to that, the suit he'd worn the day he'd killed Susan.

Above each set of clothes, he'd pinned pictures. Susan and Jo Vorster above the suit. Three more women above the MacDonalds uniform. Another above the whites. More above the other uniforms.

It was how he lured them in without anyone noticing. He camouflaged himself. He blended with his surroundings. There were twelve women on the wall, and the cops only knew about two of them. The others Zill had never seen in any file, on any wall, any database in any part of Murder and Robbery.

The others were all victims, still waiting to be found.

He backed away from the house and continued going, stumbling through bush, head thumping, nauseous, dizzy, eventually ending up back at his car. He got inside, closed the door and took a series of long, deep breaths.

Lucinda.

He removed his phone and dialled her number.

After a couple of rings she answered. Her voice was

distant, her words echoing as they travelled thousands of miles: 'Ben?'

'I've found him.'

A pause. She instantly knew who he meant.

'He's killed more.'

'More than Susan and Jo Vorster?'

'Ten more.'

Another long pause. This time, he could hear her clearing her throat. 'Ben, listen to me: I suggest you call Moses and give him the address of this guy. Let Moses go around there and bring this guy in. I don't think you should be there.'

'It's too late.'

'Why?'

'I'm already here.'

'Oh shit. Ben, what are you going to do?'

'He's high. He wouldn't know.'

'Ben –'

'He wouldn't see me coming.'

'*Ben.*'

He stopped, listening to her breath on the line.

'Ben, you asked me once, did I imagine my life turning out like this. Do you remember asking me that?'

'Yes.'

'Is this how you want *your* life to turn out?'

He didn't respond.

'Ben?'

'"I'm just a photographer."'

'What?'

'That's what *you* said to *me* once. I asked your opinion on Vorster's murder and you said to me, "I don't know. I'm just a photographer. I don't have an opinion."'

'So?'

'So maybe I feel like that too.'

'What do you mean?'

Zill looked off at the maze of broken homes. 'I don't want an opinion. I don't want people to ask me what I think when I see a young girl dumped on a railway line. I don't want to face down all the misery I see. I don't want to be a cop.'

'You do, Ben.'

'No. I don't.'

'You *do*. It's your gift.'

'No. Not now Susan is gone. Now it's my curse.'

'*Ben*. Listen to me.' She paused. 'If you do this, you're no better than him. If you do this, you go against everything you believe in. *Everything*.'

'He'll get away with it.'

'He *won't*. He'll go to prison.'

'That's what I mean.'

'Ben . . . ' A tremor of emotion sounded in her voice. 'Who are you if not a cop?'

He placed his hand on the door again, pulled at the handle and watched it pop open.

The gun shifted against his hip.

'I'm her husband.'

'Ben —'

'Goodbye, LB,' he said quietly, and ended the call.

He got out, leaving the car open, heading back through the scrub and the litter to the front of the house. The place was now in darkness. The candle was out and no light came from the window.

He tried the front door.

There was no noise as it moved on its hinges, but Zill stood there for a moment all the same, hesitating, looking into the same darkness that had stared back at him from that tape. A doorway to actions you could never take back.

There was a noise from behind him, out on the nearest road. Voices. As he listened to them, panic hit. *If I go in now, will he even be able to tell me anything?*

Zill wanted to know why.

That was what he wanted to know, above all else.

Why did he have to kill them all?

Why Susan?

Why didn't he just take her money and go?

Why did he have to take her necklace?

But then an image came back to him, of Susan, of what had been done to her, of Jo Vorster, of that abandoned railway station, and Zill realized it didn't matter. Not now. If her killer gave him no reason, *he* would at least be able to see Zill's reasons. He'd see them in Zill's face. He'd feel the gun against his head and know. Because a killer must surely recognize his reflection. He must understand the symmetry of revenge.

So, finally, Zill took another step forward.

And another.

He apologized softly.

And, slowly, he let the darkness take him away.

Hashtag, Bodybag

ALASTAIR GUNN

@Alastair_Gunn

Feeling lost without @Specsavers #Youdunnit story to think about, but can't wait to read @FrenchNicci and @TimWeaverBooks!

The marker moved onto Station Road.

She was coming.

He locked the phone and waited, subduing his exhilaration, aware that she'd soon pass his position.

It was incredible really; first that technology had advanced to the point where, with the right software, you could track someone via the GPS system on their mobile phone. And second, that most people were stupid enough to leave their privacy settings turned off.

He checked the pavement to his left, using the dentist's mirror to see without putting his head around the corner, and saw her approaching.

He withdrew the mirror, hearing a train pass in the distance, still surprised that the sound travelled all the way from the tracks half a mile north. Then again, there wasn't much around to stop the noise. Most of the old buildings on this street had been demolished to make way for redevelopment, so it didn't offer many decent hiding places. Otherwise the location was perfect: quiet, isolated, poorly lit by outdated sodium street lamps, and used by his target on a daily basis. Plus it offered this particular deserted house, near to what would be her final resting place.

He heard footsteps.

Seconds later his target passed; long auburn hair swinging halfway down her back as she walked. She didn't see him.

He let her get a few yards in front before he moved, soft-soled trainers silent on the concrete. It was only fair: she had followed him, so now he was following her. He suppressed ironic laughter.

And raised the brick.

Pete Marshall was just about perfect. That was Lucinda Berrington's assessment, at least. The news writer was tall, handsome and well-dressed, and he painted, which sat right next to her own discipline of photography in the spectrum of creative arts. Pete had done her induction at the *Saverton Star*, for the one-month freelancing contract she was currently halfway through. They'd had such a laugh that Lucinda was sure he'd ask her out afterwards. But that was nearly two weeks ago, and they hadn't exchanged a lot more than pleasantries since.

Such amorous obsession was never a good thing. The fact that Pete's desk was directly across from her own meant that Lucinda's recent work rate had been average at best. She needed to get on.

She sighed and turned back to her schedule for Wednesday: a supermarket opening, then a few clandestine shots of the roadworks on Peer Street that had overrun and weren't properly signposted. Hardly what she went to University for. At least the local eye candy improved what was otherwise the dullest place on earth. She glanced around at the poky first-floor office, at its Velcro-like carpets and woodchip wallpaper, longing for a beach. Being reduced to freelance snapper work at a struggling weekly rag in a landlocked backwater like Saverton would have been depressing enough for anyone. For a short-of-work travel photographer like Lucinda, it was purgatory.

But she was trapped.

Five years of photography at college and university, a few more in office jobs, saving hard, then a round-the-world trip designed to build her launch portfolio, had seen Lucinda return home penniless, but determined that a glittering career would follow. The trip had been amazing, but now it looked like an extravagant waste of time.

The reality, that the website she'd paid £1,000 for wasn't good enough, and that technology had moved beyond Lucinda's means in the time she'd been away, bit hard.

The recent migration of her city-based competitors to superfast internet connections meant their online portfolios were now hi-def, slick and instantly accessible. Meanwhile, Saverton's remote location between two peaky moors meant they were lucky to have running water, let alone a modern communication infrastructure. Lucinda's weedy site couldn't match the new breed, and gone were the days when you met clients in person to show your work and take contracted assignments. The only travel she'd done since joining the paper was to and from the office, and she'd had to sell her car. She'd been restricted to domestic excursions for the last six months, and money was only getting tighter, which was bad, considering she'd recently sunk a £1,000 bank loan into a new Nikon SLR.

Already twenty-eight and permanently single, Lucinda lived in a flat owned by her mum and dad, right across the road from the *Star* office. Her parents lived in France now, but they let her rent the place in Saverton for half its market value, which was nice, but it also made it difficult to justify doubling her rent by moving to a bigger town . . .

Stop feeling sorry for yourself.

Lucinda gathered her equipment and stood, about to head off for another afternoon of tedious photographic work, when a voice interrupted her thoughts.

'Lucy.' The deputy editor, Susan Masters, was heading her way. 'Hold on.'

'It's Lucinda, actually.' For the hundredth time.

Admittedly it wasn't the Susan's fault that every abbreviation of Lucinda stank. 'Sindy' was a child's toy, and 'Sinned' made her feel like she'd done something wrong. Worst of all was 'Loose', because she certainly *wasn't*.

'Lucinda,' Susan asserted, 'drop whatever you've got on this afternoon. I have a special assignment for you. Something a bit more up your street.'

Milton, the local taxi driver, pulled up on Station Road.

Lucinda paid and waited while he wrote out the receipt, still feeling naïve for having been excited by Susan's mention of a 'special assignment'.

Her instructions were to find and photograph Saverton's best 'points of interest', for a bumper edition of the paper to coincide with the coming weekend's county fair, the first time the event had been held on Saverton Common since 1984. But the only 'special' aspect of Lucinda's task was that it was now urgent, mainly because no one had got off their backside to organize it in good time.

At least it was more interesting than roadworks.

The cab driver had collected her from Saverton Waters, the lake a couple of miles outside town. People came from all over the area to partake in various water sports up there, or to enjoy the respectable panoramas over Saverton offered by the nearby hills, although its visitors rarely ended up in the town itself. Lucinda had made the most of the afternoon's clear conditions by taking a raft of shots at both sites. Unfortunately, next to that, Saverton itself offered a poor selection of sights. The local church might provide some romantic shots at dusk, but in daylight it looked like a project for a primary school joinery class, and the town hall made the church look like an architectural triumph.

She thanked Milton and climbed out, watching the taxi pull away before turning to face the last point of interest on her very short list.

Saverton railway station.

Lucinda regarded the main building through the thick wire mesh surrounding the site. Above her, a large red and white sign shouted *SAFETY RISK – DO NOT ENTER*.

The station hadn't seen passengers since it was decommissioned in the mid-nineties, due to a maintenance bill the local authority wasn't prepared to swallow. But beneath the muck and decay, the structure retained its characterful design: pleasingly symmetrical, with a taller central atrium and lower extensions on either side. A section of rusty track still ran alongside, even though this part of the line had been bypassed years earlier. The council had even talked recently about restoring the place as part of a sightseeing railway for day-trippers, so maybe Lucinda was ahead of the game.

Renovation wasn't likely to happen before the weekend, though, so she needed to capture its best side, which meant getting inside the fence.

She skirted one edge of the perimeter, looking for gaps and finding the fence disappointingly intact. She turned the corner and followed the boundary. Another undamaged run. Same story at the back. Lucinda was about to start climbing as she approached the end of the final side, but then she saw the opening. She hadn't noticed it before, because the cuts in the mesh followed a neat vertical line, and the displaced section had been folded back into place, making the hole invisible till you got near.

Lucinda paused, looking up and down the street, but there was nobody about. Buildings had once lined both pavements, but most had been knocked down after this part of the railway closed, so these days the rubble-lined road was nothing more than a thoroughfare.

She turned back to the station house. Could there be squatters? There was no noise coming from inside, and there were no signs of litter. It wasn't likely, anyway: Saverton was too small to attract many homeless people, and the community centre provided beds for those there were. Anyway, Lucinda reasoned as she pulled at the cut section, she'd be careful.

She squeezed through the gap and stood, assessing the light. The autumn sun was still pretty high and, if she backed up against the fence, she should be able to get the whole building in shot. She picked her way through the weeds to the south-west corner before snapping a few pictures, with the station's portico nicely centred.

Lucinda was heading sensibly back towards the exit when curiosity struck. She veered towards the station house, peering in through the windows.

She found herself under the porch, staring through the hole where double doors had once hung. There was still no sign of other unauthorized visitors, but Lucinda was already more interested in the ornate stucco work around the interior window frames. Pete would definitely appreciate that.

Tentatively, she placed one python-skin cowboy boot over the threshold and put all her weight on it. The building didn't fall down, so she followed up with the other foot.

From her new vantage point, Lucinda could see the small glass section set in the roof. It reminded her of Grand Central Station in New York; not on the same scale, of course, but beautiful nonetheless.

Suddenly more confident, she moved further inside, raising her camera to shoot some close-ups of the elaborate ceiling rose.

Then she tripped.

Stumbling sideways, Lucinda dropping the Nikon: 'No!'

Fortunately habit saved her, as the strap round her neck caught the heavy camera and jerked it against her hip.

Lucinda righted herself, rubbing the top of her thigh and glancing down to see what she'd fallen over.

It was a bag.

She stared at the clean fabric sack, so at odds with the station's grimy floor tiles. It couldn't have been there long. But even stranger were its contents.

Now strewn across the floor were dozens of identical key rings. Lucinda crouched and picked one up, studying it. Attached to the ring itself was what looked like a tiny bicycle chain, with ten or so miniature links in a small loop.

She reached out to pick up the next key ring, but her hand froze in mid-air.

When she saw the face.

It took a moment for her mind to process what she was seeing: two lifeless pupils staring straight back at her like a trapped owl, only feet away. Then the image registered fully, and Lucinda shot backwards into the wall, not hearing herself scream.

She slumped, breathing heavily, as her brain decoded the whole image. The strands of auburn hair strung across the cheek; the black and purple skin on the neck. The young woman was clearly dead, the angle of her limbs somehow made that obvious. But Lucinda hadn't seen her at first because the body had been sort of stuffed into the gap between a big old radiator and the corner of the building.

Lucinda edged sideways, only taking her eyes off the corpse when she was near enough to run for the door.

She struggled back through the fence and called the police.

'So you'll be OK, then?' WPC Yates asked.

'My boyfriend's coming over,' Lucinda lied, keen to be left alone, 'he'll look after me.'

She got out of the police car, hearing it drive away as she climbed the steps to her shared front door. There were four flats in the block, and unfortunately for Lucinda's weary legs, hers was at the top.

She drifted up the first flight of stairs, reassuring herself that she'd told the police everything she'd seen at the station. They'd all been captivated by her story and hadn't seemed bothered at all about her having trespassed. But that wasn't surprising; it was unlikely anyone had *ever* been murdered in Saverton before. The resident police were more used to dealing with disputes over the heights of people's garden hedges. Homicide was horrid, the officers had all agreed, but Lucinda recognized the excitement in everyone's eyes.

Real police work for a change.

She reached the top landing and unlocked her front door. She stepped inside and was almost knocked over by her black Border Collie.

'Bloody hell, Sam,' she heaved the dog off her and bent down to give him a hug, 'I'm soooo, sorry, darling. You must be starved.'

'I can make it up to you, though,' she walked through into the kitchen, with Sam close behind. She began searching her bag: 'I bought you some of that yummy packet dog food today.'

At the mention of his favourite word, Sam immediately assumed the Crufts position: bolt upright, stock still, eyes on owner. He'd never been to a dog show, but Lucinda often wondered what would happen if she took him to one. Sam was mainly white, but the patches of black on his flanks and over one eye were unbroken and beautifully shaped, as if someone had designed him to look good. She really needed to get a house with a garden for him.

Lucinda's attention was suddenly elsewhere, as her hand found something that certainly shouldn't have been in her bag. Oblivious to Sam's whimpering, she pulled the item out.

The key ring she'd picked up at the railway station; she still had it. Her mind flashed back to when the police had arrived at the scene. The female officer had prised it from her stupefied grasp and put it in her bag, obviously assuming that whatever it was belonged to her, and Lucinda had forgotten all about it until now.

She'd removed evidence from a crime scene.

Then she remembered there had been dozens of the things, so one less wouldn't make any immediate difference. She'd return it with an apology when she had the chance.

She took a deep breath, fed her almost apoplectic dog, and made herself some dinner.

Thursday morning promised to turn into the brightest day of the week, with unseasonably warm sunlight streaming through Lucinda's open window as she clattered around the bedroom, getting ready for work. At least the chaos kept images of the dead woman's stare from her mind.

As usual, Sam watched the proceedings from the bed, while the television in the corner showed the breakfast news. The headlines were full of political nonsense and stuff about inflation, but Lucinda killed the hairdryer when the reporter handed over to Saverton's regional news station.

The picture cut straight to Tim Donoghue, the local channel's whitest-toothed frontman, who had obviously made an effort for national TV. His improbably abundant hair was quiffed even higher than usual, and he was obviously suppressing the irreverent style he got away with in front of a smaller audience. He stood outside the railings Lucinda had negotiated the previous afternoon.

She turned up the volume as Tim began talking.

'Thanks, Kate. I'm at Saverton railway station. As you can see behind me, the station itself is now derelict, but detectives are currently in the main building because, yesterday afternoon, the body of a local woman was discovered here. Police have just confirmed the victim was twenty-seven-year-old Jo Kinnock, a mature student at Plymouth University. Jo had returned home for the summer break, but was about to go back for the new semester. Investigators say she was attacked right where I'm standing at some point on Tuesday evening, knocked unconscious and then dragged inside, where she was strangled to death.'

Donoghue concluded by saying that police were still looking into the murder, and then handed back to the studio. Lucinda shuddered as the victim's eyes flashed through her mind again, and went back to drying her hair.

'Hi,' he held out a hand, 'so you're Lucinda?'

'Yeah,' she shook it, noting the coarseness of his skin. So this was Ian Beck, the boy from Saverton done good. Beck had been a local hero for as long as she could remember, but these days he was becoming an international superstar, who was increasingly referred to as 'the new Bradley Wiggins'.

He was a little wiry for Lucinda's taste, and not exactly tall, but he definitely had charisma, with sculpted shades perfectly placed in his spiky blonde hair, and expensive, sponsorship-peppered clothing. A gang of PR and security people hovered nearby.

Lucinda had arrived late that morning, just in time to catch the end of the editor's announcement that Beck was coming in after lunch. The cyclist was in town on some sort of promotional drive, and had agreed to be interviewed by the *Star*'s editor in chief, Justin Wake. Normally a reporter would have gone to Beck, but apparently Justin had persuaded him to come in and meet his 'very excited' staff, although Lucinda suspected Justin's motives were purely selfish. Perhaps with the exception of Pete, the rest of the office looked like they couldn't have cared less.

Beck interrupted her thoughts, perching on the edge of her desk and lowering his tone, 'Sorry to disturb your work, but I heard about what happened yesterday, and I just wanted to meet you and ... offer my condolences. Did you know the victim?'

Lucinda shook her head.

'I'm visiting the family later on,' he volunteered. 'They're distraught, obviously, but it must have been terrible, finding the body like that.'

'It isn't something I'm keen to repeat.'

He nodded in deliberate fashion, then changed the subject, 'So, what do you do here?'

'Just freelance snapper work, but I'm actually a travel photographer.'

'Right,' his eyebrows raised. 'What does that entail?'

'Globetrotting, when I can afford it, taking beautiful pictures to sell when I get home.'

'Sounds excellent.' He smiled, just as they were interrupted by one of his entourage.

'Come on, Ian.' The suited young guy said in a soft London accent. 'People to see, yeah?'

'All right,' Beck stood. 'Lucinda, this is my publicist, Dean Bradstock.'

Bradstock gave her a derisive nod. 'You found the dead girl, then?'

Lucinda nodded.

'Bad luck,' he said, already shepherding Beck away. 'Sorry to drag him away, love, but we're behind. I'll sort you out a signed poster or something.'

And with that the two men retreated towards Beck's management team, before they all disappeared into Justin's office.

Lucinda sat for a moment, wondering if she'd be known for evermore as 'the girl who found the body'. She removed her glasses and massaged her temples. She wasn't a great sleeper at the best of times, but yesterday's discovery had kept her awake half the night. She could have used a sympathetic ear, but she hadn't been at the paper long enough to make any proper friends, and her three best mates were on holiday together in Corfu. They'd offered to club together to buy her a ticket, but she hadn't let them. She couldn't even afford the time off.

Her head shot up when the day's second surprise visitor spoke.

'You lucky cow. What did he say?

Pete.

She gazed up at Mr Right, 'Er, he wanted to know about the body.'

'Course.' Pete looked mildly disappointed, 'Are you OK?'

'Oh yeah,' she waved his question away. 'How are you?'

'I'm cool, except I have to write a follow-up piece on the murder for tomorrow's front page, and I've got bugger all.'

He paused as Lucinda nodded, tongue-tied but willing him to stay.

Suddenly his face lit up, 'Hey, what am I thinking . . . you were *there*, right? You must've seen *something* that wasn't mentioned in the news today.'

Her mind went blank.

All she could think about was how nice his shoulders were and how good his aftershave smelled. The moment stretched, and Pete's expression clouded as she stared blankly at him. He mumbled something about never minding and began to move away.

Suddenly Lucinda's memory spurred itself and she blurted out the words, surprising them both. 'Key rings.'

'What?' he turned back.

'Key rings,' she repeated. 'There was a bag full of them near the body.' Frantically searching her pockets.

Pete fetched a chair from the next desk and sat down. 'What sort of key rings?'

'They were all exactly like this.' She found the one she still had and handed it to him. 'Dozens of them in a bag on the floor of the station. I guess they were the victim's.'

'OK,' Pete turned it over in his hands. 'Why would she have loads of Ian Beck key rings?'

'Ian Beck?' Lucinda asked without thinking.

'Blimey,' Pete smirked. 'You really *aren't* a fan, are you? Beck won the Tour of Britain last month, so they've invited him to be guest of honour at the county fair this weekend.' He held up the key ring, 'Didn't pick up on the bicycle-chain thing, then?'

She blushed. 'No.'

'Fair enough.' He shrugged. 'It's a replica of the prototype chain Beck used when he won a couple of stages in the Tour de France. Thanks, Lucy; this might be exactly what I need.'

He settled back in his chair as Lucinda considered changing her name.

'Pete.' Susan Masters appeared, smashing their new-found rapport, 'Why are you still here? You're meeting the local MP at the town hall in ten minutes.'

Pete checked his watch and swore. 'Sorry, boss. Leaving right now.'

They both watched Masters retreat huffily to her desk.

'Look,' Pete said when she was out of earshot, 'I'll be tied up for the rest of the afternoon with this rubbish, but I really want to hear about what happened yesterday. Why don't you come to mine about eight-ish and tell me the whole story? I'll make you dinner.'

'OK.' Lucinda tried not to sound too eager. 'Where do you live?'

He scribbled the address on a Post-it before heading for the stairs. Lucinda watched him all the way, already thinking about what she was going to wear.

For their date.

Lucinda's selection turned out to be light blue jeans and her favourite paisley patterned shirt with the huge collar, topped off with a fake-fur body warmer and, of course, her python-skin boots. She'd even broken out her FCUK glasses with the red frames, which were reserved for properly special occasions.

It had been the first outfit she'd thought of, before trying five others and then reverting to her original choice.

She might have looked a little quirky, but this was how she felt comfortable. And tonight was all about being herself.

It was already dark – the autumn nights were closing in – so she stuck to the main roads, where the lighting was better. It took fifteen minutes to walk from her place to Pete's, which was in the newer part of town.

Kensington Street actually lived up to its rather grand name, with low manicured hedges lining fashionably tiny front gardens. There was no way Pete could have afforded one on whatever the paper paid him, which meant he either had another source of income or wealthy parents. As she arrived at the door of number eight, Lucinda decided she didn't really mind either way.

Pete's house was an end of terrace, with a front door set into the side wall, halfway between the front and rear gardens. She wandered up and rang the bell, hearing it *ding dong* from inside. She took a deep breath and let it out, jigging on the step to relax her nerves.

Had she made too much effort?

She began to panic, picturing Pete coming to the door in ripped jeans and a scruffy old T-shirt, and spent the next few seconds concocting a story about having a party to go to afterwards. Then she rejected the idea, realizing that if things went well, he might want to come with her.

You look fine. You look like you. Just be cool.

Lucinda jigged some more, watching the frosted panel beside the door for signs of movement. She reassured herself that she had actually rung the bell, resisting the urge to ring again, but Pete *was* taking a long time, and she was starving.

She walked back to the pavement and checked the

window; there was definitely a light on. She looked at the cars lining the street. She didn't even know if Pete drove, but pretty much any of them could have been his.

She returned to the door, looking at her watch. The hands above Salvador Dali's moustache said it was bang on eight. Was she being stood up? Did people do that at their own houses?

Lucinda dismissed the idea. He'd invited her over to talk about a story, something he needed her help with. Surely he wouldn't have done that if he wanted to avoid her. Either he'd been delayed with the work thing, or there'd been some sort of emergency. She realized they hadn't exchanged numbers, mobile or home, so she couldn't ring, but neither was she going to wait on the doorstep all night.

She decided to leave a note.

Lucinda plumbed her bag for a piece of paper and scribbled a note to say she could come back if it wasn't too late, adding her number, then she bent down to post it through the letterbox. But as she pushed at the flap, the door moved inwards.

It was on the latch.

She glanced back at the street, unsure what to do. Perhaps she should go and fetch a neighbour. Or maybe Pete was in need of assistance and every second counted.

She held her breath and pushed the door. It swung inwards, revealing a neat hallway with stairs leading off to her right. Beyond the banisters, an open door revealed a sliver of kitchen.

'Hello?' Lucinda called as she stepped inside. 'Pete?'

Her heart pounded as she closed the door behind her,

glancing through the archway to her left. Two small leather sofas faced each other over a dark wood coffee table, but there was no sign of Pete. She looked in the kitchen. Empty as well.

'It's Lucinda,' she shouted, moving towards the stairs. 'Anybody home?'

She began to climb. It felt really odd being alone in someone's house, but something had to be wrong.

The stairs turned back on themselves halfway up – an attractive feature that Lucinda would have admired under normal circumstances – but as she reached the landing, her attention was on the three remaining doors. The first was open, revealing what was obviously Pete's bedroom. She checked the floor behind the bed, in case he'd passed out in a diabetic coma or something, but he wasn't there.

In the middle was the bathroom, similarly deserted. But the final door, most likely a spare room, was closed.

Lucinda approached slowly, aware that if there *was* anyone here, they were in this room. She almost chickened out, but after a moment's deliberation, and with her heart beating loud in her ears, Lucinda gripped the handle, opened the door.

And saw him.

She froze in the doorway as the air dropped out of her lungs. Pete was sitting in an office chair, facing away, slumped forwards on a desk under the window. He wasn't moving, but Lucinda didn't approach him.

Because she'd seen the blood.

The compact desk was covered in it; a shiny pool that dripped off the edges here and there; stretchy filaments abseiling gracefully down onto the oat-coloured carpet.

The puddle was broken only by a laptop computer, a ring-bound notepad and Pete.

Lucinda swallowed, realizing she should check his pulse.

It might not be as bad as it looked.

She fought to control her breathing as she stepped forwards, trying not to make any noise, although she wasn't sure why. She reached the desk, assessing Pete's condition. There was a large dent in the back of his head, where he'd obviously been hit, and Lucinda brought a hand to her mouth, partly to stop herself from bursting into tears; mostly to keep from throwing up.

She wasn't sure where you felt someone's neck for a pulse, so she opted for a wrist. Pete's right arm was resting on the desk, right in the pool of blood, but his left arm hung straight down, so Lucinda crouched next to him and, with shaking fingers, gripped it just above the hand.

Nothing.

She released it, chewing her bottom lip as the tears started. Suddenly she leaned closer, confused by the familiar shape she'd noticed on the floor under the desk.

A bicycle-chain key ring.

She reached out and picked it up, examining the small plastic object more closely than she had before. Just like the original, it had a small red tag attached to the ring, but until now she hadn't read the words printed on it in white letters. It looked like a Twitter address.

@iLoveIanBeck.

Was it the same key ring?

She tried to picture exactly what had happened earlier in the day, when she'd shown her key ring to Peter. She hadn't thought about it at the time, but now she was sure he hadn't given it back.

Lucinda replaced the key ring where she'd found it, not wanting to remove evidence from a second successive crime scene, and slowly made her way downstairs.

She lowered herself slowly onto one of Pete's sofas and rang the police.

Again.

Lucinda spent Friday at home.

The police had called her boss, Justin, the previous night, to inform him that one of his journalists had been murdered and that his temporary photographer had found the body.

Later on, after the same WPC had dropped her home, and she'd told the same lie about a boyfriend being around, Justin had called Lucinda to say she didn't have to go in the following day. He'd even offered to pay her, which was the only reason she'd accepted, even though she now wished she hadn't.

She had spent the whole day indoors, ignoring Sam's pleas for walkies; too scared to leave the flat in case she tripped over another corpse, wondering what kind of deity she must have insulted. The odds of finding *one* dead body in a town as small and tranquil as Saverton were negligible, but for a single resident to find two bodies in as many days was beyond ridiculous.

What the hell was going on?

She buzzed around the kitchen, putting the finishing touches to the pasta Bolognese she'd made for dinner, thinking about Pete. She had hoped that cooking, which normally demanded her full attention, might take her mind off the whole horrid situation. But her naturally inquisitive mind kept trying to work out what had happened.

She had the TV on, partly as another distraction, but also because she wanted to catch the next update about the murders. The national news came on just as she was dishing up. She left her plate half loaded and drifted closer to the screen, startled to see her latest discovery topping the bill.

'The headlines at six,' the presenter said. 'Another murder in Saverton.'

Lucinda sank onto a chair as the other headlines were read out. She'd avoided earlier reports because they made Pete's death seem more real somehow, but she couldn't ignore it for ever. She made herself watch as the newsreader reappeared.

'Two days ago, twenty-seven-year-old Jo Kinnock was murdered in the small Somerset town of Saverton. But police are now investigating a second killing that happened last night, less than half a mile from the scene of the first attack. Our correspondent is at the scene now. Tim, what's the latest?'

The image changed. Tim Donoghue stood at the end of the road Lucinda recognized from the previous night. Pete's road.

'Thanks, Margaret.' The reporter motioned towards the property. 'I'm here in Saverton, just south of Bristol. The town has a population of a few thousand, and certainly isn't accustomed to incidents of this nature, so locals were shocked when Jo Kinnock was murdered not far from here on Wednesday night. But last night a second local resident, a journalist who worked at the town's paper, was bludgeoned to death in his home office. Of course a police investigation is already underway, and I'm joined now by Superintendent Maurice Pike of Saverton police.'

The camera panned out to reveal a uniformed policeman; evidently the nearest thing Saverton had to a resident detective.

Donoghue continued: 'Thanks for joining us, Superintendent. So what can you tell us about last night's events?'

'Well,' Pike looked nervous, 'none of the neighbours witnessed anyone approaching the property, prior to the person who found the body, that is, so we believe Mr Marshall's attacker came across the fields that run right up to the rear of these houses. The assailant jimmied the front door lock, apparently without alerting the victim. Forensic evidence suggests Mr Marshall died at around 7 p.m. yesterday, approximately an hour before his body was discovered.'

Lucinda's heart leapt. Sixty minutes earlier and she'd have walked in on the murderer.

'Two deaths in less than twenty-four hours,' Donoghue continued. 'This is becoming something of a crisis, isn't it?'

'Definitely not.' Pike's reply was obviously intended to reassure, but his voice faltered. 'It's still early days, and our investigators are making solid progress.'

Donoghue nodded, 'Do you have sufficient resources to handle a case of this type?'

'Saverton has a small resident force,' Pike said, 'but additional resources are being sent over by neighbouring departments.'

'Is there anything else you'd like to say to the public?'

Pike's tone was more confident as he faced the camera. 'I personally guarantee that every possible avenue will be investigated. So if anyone has information regarding either murder, no matter how insignificant it might seem, they should call the inquiry number provided by Somerset police.'

Donoghue thanked the superintendent as the camera turned back to him, cutting the policeman out of shot. He read out the hotline number, reiterated the situation's gravity, and said the news channel would keep viewers up to date with developments, then he handed back to the studio.

Lucinda muted the television, deep in thought. What the superintendent obviously hadn't wanted to say was that, if the killer had struck twice in as many days, they might do it again. Soon.

The police needed all the help they could get. She finished serving up and slowly ate, racking her brains for anything she hadn't told them. But nothing came.

She stood to deposit her empty plate in the sink just as the local news took over, and another familiar face appeared. She turned the volume back up.

Unusually, Saverton was in the news again, but this time not because of the murders. Ian Beck and his surly publicist, Dean, stood on Saverton Common, in front of a part-constructed fairground ride.

'I was honoured to be asked.' The cyclist beamed. 'Of course it's amazing to win big events, but there's nothing like coming back to my home town and seeing the people who helped me get started in the sport. I hope the whole of south-east England turns up at the county fair tomorrow. It's going to be a great event.'

As she watched the star's face on the TV, Lucinda suddenly remembered the notepad on Pete's desk. The police told her it had been covered with facts about the cyclist, and had asked Lucinda if she knew why that might have been. She'd suggested that Pete had probably been working on a piece for the next edition of the paper, to coincide with Beck's appearance at the fair, but now it occurred to her that perhaps there might have been another explanation.

Were the murders connected in some way to Ian Beck?

The miniature bike chains she'd seen at both murder scenes were designed to promote Beck's impending appearance at the county fair, and Pete had obviously been investigating the cyclist when he was killed.

Then she remembered the Twitter address.

She grabbed her bag and fished out her mobile, opening the social media app, trying to recall the exact phrase printed on the tag attached to the key ring.

Slowly she typed *@iLoveIanBeck* and hit 'Search'.

After a few seconds one result appeared and she tapped to view it. It looked like she'd remembered it correctly, because a picture of the cyclist appeared. Apart from that, the account looked suspiciously new. It had made a single tweet, saying simply *#DieHardBeckFan*, it wasn't following anyone and had only two followers of its own.

Lucinda tapped to see who was following *@iLoveIanBeck*, recoiling when she saw the two names.

Jo Kinnock. Pete Marshall.

Both the killer's victims.

Lucinda's mind raced. OK, so it was no surprise that Jo had been following the feed as she'd had a bag full of the key rings promoting that very address. And Pete must have followed the account after Lucinda had shown him the key ring. But was it really possible they were killed simply *because* they'd followed the account?

It was too much of a coincidence to ignore.

She rang the police straight away and told the operator about her discovery. She made him promise to pass the information directly to Superintendent Pike and rang off. But instead of feeling unburdened, Lucinda couldn't escape the thought that she should be doing more.

She sat in her kitchen, thinking about Jo, Pete and Ian Beck. Could Pete have been killed because he was investigating the cyclist, or the Twitter account? Or both?

There was only one way to find out.

Lucinda grabbed her bag and headed for the door, promising Sam that she'd walk him later. She rushed downstairs and left the apartment block. Within minutes she was at work.

Lucinda used her key to open the door, re-locking it behind her. It was 6:45 p.m. on Friday evening, so it was unlikely anyone else would still be at their desk.

She climbed the stairs to the first floor and scanned the office for anyone working late. She even checked Justin's office, but there was no one around. Satisfied that she had the place to herself, Lucinda walked slowly towards Pete's desk.

It felt really odd standing there. She hadn't known him that well, admittedly, but it was still hard to believe he was dead. Her guts twisted when she remembered the moment she'd found him.

Concentrate.

She took a deep breath and sat down at the desk, switching on his computer.

While she waited for the system to load, Lucinda searched the piles of paper and magazines on Pete's desk, but nothing offered any clues. Next she turned her attention to his PC.

She had noticed on the morning of her induction that Pete didn't use a password on his PC, even though Susan Masters spent her life telling everyone they should, and she was relieved to see he hadn't subsequently listened to their editor, as his desktop appeared.

Lucinda opened the Internet browser and checked the history. There were hundreds of sites, and the last couple of dozen were all related to Beck. She checked each one, but they were just old news stories about his multiple victories and prolific recent form.

She minimized the window and used the search function to look for files containing the words 'Ian' or 'Beck' on the hard drive. It found the original article about Jo Kinnock, plus some early drafts for Pete's follow-up piece, but none contained anything sinister.

Then Lucinda spent half an hour clicking into his folders one at a time, looking for anything else that might have been connected. Still nothing.

She closed everything down, convinced she was wasting her time. But just as she was about to log off, an icon in the corner of the desktop caught her eye.

IB-Jul-09

She opened it, noticing that the shortcut linked to a file

on the paper's main server. She hadn't thought to check there because she had never been given access. But Pete's system must have had the password saved, because the file opened and she began to read.

It was a scanned article from the *Star* itself, dated 11 July 2009, with the headline: BECK OFF! The image, possibly taken during a race, showed a glaring Ian Beck, but the copy alleged that the cyclist had been so furious after losing in the final stage of a British championship race in Dorset that he'd attacked one of his fans in the car park afterwards. Lucinda read the whole thing twice, but her amazement peaked only when she recognized the name of the person who had written the article.

Tim Donoghue.

She sat for a moment, wondering how many Tim Donoghues there could be in Saverton. Could the television presenter really have worked for the *Star*? Then she realized it wasn't all that unlikely that the reporter's news-focused career would have started at a local paper.

Perhaps she could ask him?

Lucinda reached for Pete's Rolodex. The writer had spent years building a contacts list in the area, so it wasn't unrealistic that he might have a direct number for Donoghue.

He did.

Lucinda propped the Rolodex open at the right place and pulled the desk phone towards her, considering whether to look for more files on the server first. But if Pete had found this one, it was logical he would also have looked for others, which made it likely this article was the only one.

She picked up the handset, dialled the mobile number

and listened to the line buzz as her call connected. At last it began to ring.

He answered quickly: 'Donoghue.'

'Mr Donoghue.' Lucinda tried to sound like a journalist. 'My name is Lucinda Berrington, and I'm with the *Saverton Star*. I'd like to ask you about an article you wrote when you worked for the paper in 2009.'

'Really?' he sounded suspicious. 'In the office rather late, aren't you? I thought all you journalist types were half-cut in the Woolpack by seven on Fridays.'

'It's an important case. Two people have been murdered.' She hoped he wouldn't ask for more details. Research was normally done by reporters; not the travel photographer.

'And which article would that be exactly?'

He *had* worked for the paper. 'The one about Ian Beck attacking a fan.'

'Ah,' Donoghue said. 'I don't think I should stir that particular pot at the moment. Thanks for your call.'

'Wait,' Lucinda called. 'What if we traded information?'

There was silence for a few seconds, but the background noise on the line suggested he hadn't hung up. It sounded like he was driving.

Eventually he replied, 'Go on.'

She told him about Peter investigating the cyclist just before he was killed, that she had found both the bodies, the key rings, and what she suspected about the Twitter address.

Another pause. 'Who else knows about this?'

'No one.' Lucinda was getting into the reassuring journalist role. 'It's all strictly off the record.'

That seemed to do the trick.

'All right,' Donoghue said. 'But this goes no further unless I say. There are court orders involved.'

'OK,' she agreed, having nothing to lose. 'So how did you know about Beck attacking the fan?'

'I was there, covering the event for the *Star*. I saw it happen, even though Beck's denied it ever since. The victim was only a kid, fifteen or so. He waited by Beck's car after the event for an autograph, but Beck punched him in the face and drove off. I didn't think he should get away with it, so I wrote the story.'

'So if you witnessed it, how did he get off?'

'It was all hushed up by his lawyers. They knew he was about to hit the big time, so they threw the book at us.'

'And you let it go?'

'I tried to follow up on it,' Donoghue said, 'but Beck's promoters couldn't afford blemishes on his record. Their lawyers turned up at the paper within hours; came down on the editor like an anvil, tying him up in so many legal knots that we couldn't afford to print further allegations. They even made him print a retraction. And I got released from my contract.'

'Could it have been an isolated incident, Beck just having a bad day?'

'I wondered that, so I did some digging afterwards. The rumour among Beck's peers was that he couldn't stand his fans, especially the really keen ones. He used to joke about having them taken out.'

Lucinda couldn't believe her ears. 'You have to go to the police,' she told him. 'They need to know about this.'

Donoghue's tone hardened. 'I told you, this goes no further.'

'People are dying.'

'It doesn't make sense anyway. Why would Beck risk it? He might not like his fans, but he'd have to be insane to start murdering them.'

'Maybe,' she countered, 'but there's plenty of evidence worth exploring. And what if someone else dies tonight? If you don't want to tell the police, I can do it. I'll just say I found the article and they'll investigate.'

There was a moment's silence before Donoghue let out a long sigh. 'OK, maybe you're right. I'll call them straight after. But don't say I didn't warn you if all legal hell breaks loose.'

Lucinda thanked him, said he was doing the right thing and rang off. She emailed a copy of the article to herself, gathered her belongings and switched off the lights, feeling like she'd done her civic duty.

It was only on her way down the stairs that she realized Donoghue could have been lying.

What if he'd only said he'd ring the police to get rid of her?

Deciding it was best to make sure, Lucinda pulled out her phone and scrolled to the inquiry hotline number she'd copied off the television earlier on. She'd call on her way home. Even if Donoghue denied having the conversation with her, she still had the article.

Lucinda reached the bottom of the steps, unlocked the main door and stepped onto the pavement. According to her phone it was already half past nine, and the streets at the quiet end of town were dark and deserted. She was about to turn back to lock the door when she saw the silhouette.

Someone was standing in the shadows at the end of the path.

'Hello?' Lucinda said.

For a second the silhouette didn't respond, but then it moved, leaving the shadows and coming towards her. She squinted through the darkness, startled when she recognized her mystery visitor.

Tim Donoghue.

'What are you doing here?' she asked, startled by how much older the presenter looked in person. It had been just minutes since they'd finished talking on the phone.

'Not outside,' Donoghue grabbed her by the arm and manoeuvred her back into the building, closing the door behind them. 'Lock it,' he ordered.

'Why?' Lucinda demanded. 'What's going on?'

'Look, there's more to this whole thing than you've realized.' Donoghue took the keys off her and locked the door. 'I guessed you'd be here, so I came straight over. We need to talk. Please?'

'All right.' She led him up to the office and turned. 'You need to tell me what this is—'

Light flashed across Lucinda's vision as the fist crashed into her jaw. She sprawled into the nearest desk, looking up to see Donoghue advancing.

He grabbed her by the neck and dragged her across to a chair, dumping her in it. 'That's what you get for sticking your mindless nose in other people's business.'

Lucinda's jaw was singing, but she managed to talk. 'Why are you doing this?'

Donoghue laughed. 'You really aren't very bright, are you?' He dug a hand inside his jacket, and Lucinda noticed for the first time that he was wearing gloves.

He produced a knife, 'I'm doing this because I can't have you digging up the past before I'm ready.'

Lucinda's blood ran cold as she stared at the blade. 'Did you . . .'

'Kill Jo and your friend, Pete? Actually I did.' He cocked his head. 'Oops, that was careless. Now I have to murder you, too.'

'But . . .' Lucinda blinked hard, trying to clear her head. She had to keep him talking. 'Why?'

'Well, where to start?' Donoghue pulled up a second chair and sat in front of her, holding the knife between them, apparently happy to talk. 'OK, how about this. Here's Tim Donoghue, forty years old next Tuesday, working at some crummy local TV station, when a few years ago I was being tipped for national television. But why, when I used to be the biggest star ever to come out of this fetid little town? Everything was going well for me: guest of honour here, opening day care centres there, the lot. Then along comes this idiot, born and bred in Saverton, and he starts winning international cycling events. Well, everybody just loves that, don't they? All of a sudden it's: *Tim who?* I tried to take him down a peg or two with the story about him attacking a fan, but his swanky lawyers managed to kill that and ruin me in the process. So I end up playing to the blue-rinse brigade on boondocks TV, while he's just passed a million followers on Twitter. He owes me, big time.'

'So if Beck's the problem,' she said, realizing he was keen to tell his story, 'why murder Jo and Pete?'

Donoghue frowned, as if the answer was obvious. 'Because they followed *@iloveIanBeck*, of course.'

He reached into his pocket, producing one of the bicycle-chain key rings, 'I set up the Twitter address and had these made for tomorrow's fair, and I'm going to kill anyone stupid enough to follow it. But it seems Jo didn't deliver them to the fair's organizers like I'd asked. Don't worry, though, I've ordered some more.'

The ringing in Lucinda's ears had eased a little, and she scanned the desk for anything she could use to defend herself.

Donoghue followed her eyes. 'Don't,' he warned. 'I'm bigger and stronger than you are.'

'So you kill a few of his supporters.' Lucinda looked back at him. 'What then?'

'Then we'll find out what Mr Wonderful's fans are *really* worth to him.' Donoghue waved the knife at her. 'Plus I get some long overdue exposure by being front man on all the national news reports. I have to admit, though, I never thought of framing him for killing them himself. That's genius. How did you come up with it?'

She ignored his question. 'Why wait all these years?'

'Because he had to be here, in town. If this happened when he was on the other side of the planet, how would I know he'd see? I had to wait for the right time.'

But as he finished his sentence, the distraction Lucinda had been stalling for arrived.

Donoghue's phone rang.

He glanced down, just for a second, but it was enough.

Lucinda's hand shot out; grabbing the scissors she had seen in the pen pot on the desk, and rammed them, point down, into Donoghue's right foot.

He screamed and dropping to a crouch, pulling the implement free.

In those few seconds Lucinda shot off her chair, picked up the large fire extinguisher from beside the desk, and brought it down as hard as she could on the top of Donoghue's head. There was a dull metallic thunk, and the reporter slumped sideways, a bloodstain growing steadily on his tan leather shoe.

Lucinda discarded the extinguisher, breathing hard, noting the head-shaped dent in its tough metal casing. Donoghue looked like he was out cold, but it was best to be sure. She ran to her desk and found the bungee cords she used to stabilize her tripods on windy days, and bound his hands and feet.

She finished and stood, ready to call the police, but another noise interrupted her. Donoghue's phone was ringing again. She searched his pockets and pulled it free.

The number was withheld. It occurred to her that he might have had an accomplice. The call could be from anyone, anywhere, but perhaps she could fool them for long enough to at least find out who they were. She pressed the button to answer the call, careful as she brought the phone to her ear not to make any noises that would inform the other person they were speaking to a woman.

'It's me,' the caller said after a moment.

Lucinda slowly sank onto her office chair, shocked. This voice was familiar, too. It sounded like Ian Beck.

There was a pause. She breathed louder, hoping he could hear.

'You win,' Beck said at last. 'I didn't believe you'd go through with it at first, but now I do.'

Lucinda's brain raced to catch up with what was happening. Could he really be talking about the murders?

She tuned back in as he continued: 'You can have your half million; I'll transfer it to your account tomorrow. But then this thing's done, OK? Just don't kill anyone else.'

Lucinda ended the call and lowered the phone, as the truth became clear in her mind. Donoghue had been blackmailing Beck, obviously having threatened the cyclist's fans. It looked like Beck had called his bluff, but the reporter had actually been prepared to kill. Which meant Beck had known about the murders, if not before Jo's, then definitely before Peter's. And for whatever reason – probably because he hadn't wanted the negative publicity – he'd done nothing about it until two people were dead. She stood for a few seconds, thinking.

And then she called the police.

Saturday afternoon was like summer.

The county fair was a big success, Saverton Common practically overflowed with visitors from all over the south-west of England. The brightly coloured stands and packed fairground rides bathed in the unusually warm autumn weather. And everyone seemed just a bit friendlier than normal.

Or perhaps it was simply collective relief.

Obviously the only subject of conversation was minor local celebrity and TV news reporter Tim Donoghue, who had been arrested the previous night for the murders of Pete Marshall and Jo Kinnock.

There was tangible disappointment when it was announced that, due to unforeseen personal circumstances, Ian Beck was unable to attend, but his eight-year-old niece accepted the achievement award on his behalf. Poor kid.

Lucinda watched the presentation with sympathy, aware that, for now, she was the only person at the fair who knew almost the full story. There was no point spoiling anyone else's afternoon, though; they'd find out soon enough.

Her three best friends were due to arrive home from Corfu that afternoon, but Lucinda fully expected to be explaining her own story long before she got to see any of their holiday snaps.

After listening to Beck's enlightening call to Tim Donoghue, Lucinda had rung the police. They'd arrived at the *Star* offices within moments, before the murderous television presenter had even stirred. Apparently she'd done no permanent damage, although Lucinda still couldn't decide whether she considered that a good thing or not.

Once she'd explained her evening to Inspector Pike, Ian Beck had been arrested on charges of perverting the course of justice. When questioned, he'd admitted that Donoghue had threatened to start killing his fans if he didn't transfer half a million pounds directly to his blackmailer's account. He'd called the reporter's bluff, but realized the strategy had backfired when he saw Jo Kinnock had been killed. At that point he knew coming clean would have implicated him, so he'd just buried his head, hoping that Donoghue would chicken out and disappear.

Obviously that hadn't been the case. The irony was that by trying to protect his reputation rather than the lives of his supporters, by knowing about the murders in advance and doing nothing to stop them, Beck had practically guaranteed his career was over.

Donoghue was still refusing to admit killing the two victims, but the police said that with Lucinda's testimony, and forensics working hard on the two previous scenes, they'd soon have all the evidence necessary to put him away for a very long time.

The conclusion that Lucinda reached, as she wandered across to join her colleagues from the paper, was that fame could be a dangerous pursuit.

Blindly followed by some.

SHOULD'VE GONE TO SPECSAVERS

This novella is a unique collaboration between crime fans and bestselling authors, brought together by Specsavers and Penguin. Contributors to #YouDunnit on Twitter suggested story ideas, characters, crimes and locations for Nicci French, Tim Weaver and debut novelist Alistair Gunn to craft into this brand new work of fiction.

Proud sponsor of The Crime Thriller Awards

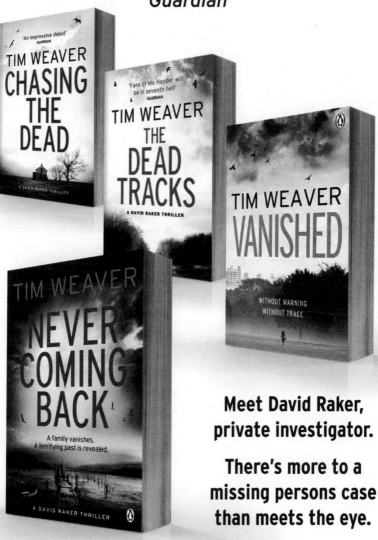

ALASTAIR GUNN

THE COUNTDOWN TO CHRISTMAS HAS NEVER BEEN THIS TERRIFYING

AVAILABLE FROM NOVEMBER 2014